Text Classics

T0363044

ELEANOR SPENCE was born in 1928 in Sydney. She grew up on her parents' orange orchard in Erina on the central New South Wales coast, and went to Gosford High School and then Sydney University. After graduating, she worked as a teacher and a librarian in Australia and later for a time in the UK.

Although she had started writing stories as a young child, it was only when she realised that there were very few books set in Australia for Australian children that she began writing seriously. Eleanor's first novel, *Patterson's Track*, which was based on rural life in Erina, was published in 1958, and she went on to write twenty-three books for children, almost all set in New South Wales.

Several of her novels were written in the 1960s when her three children, Nigel, Alister and Lisette, were very young. Her third novel, *Lillipilly Hill*, published in 1960, looked at family life in rural Australia in the late nineteenth century and was among her first to touch on social issues.

The Green Laurel and *The October Child* were awarded the Children's Book Council of Australia's book of the year. *The October Child* was also shortlisted for Britain's prestigious Carnegie Medal.

In 1998 Eleanor received an Emeritus Fellowship from the Australia Council and in 2006 she was awarded Member of the Order of Australia for services to children's literature. She died in Erina in 2008.

URSULA DUBOSARSKY was born in Sydney in 1961. She has written more than thirty books for children and young adults, including the award-winning novels *The Golden Day* and *The Red Shoe* and the acclaimed non-fiction titles *The Word Spy* and *The Return of the Word Spy*. Ursula lives in Sydney with her husband and three children.

ALSO BY ELEANOR SPENCE

Patterson's Track
The Summer in Between
The Green Laurel
The Year of the Currawong
The Switherby Pilgrims
Jamberoo Road
A Schoolmaster
A Cedar-Cutter
The Nothing Place
Time to go Home
The Travels of Hermann
The October Child
A Candle for St Antony
The Seventh Pebble
The Left Overs
Me and Jeshua
Miranda Going Home
Mary and Frances: A Story about Mary MacKillop and the Sisters of St Joseph
Deezle Boy
Another October Child: Recollections of Eleanor Spence
The Family Book of Mary Claire
Another Sparrow Singing

Lillipilly Hill
Eleanor Spence

Text Publishing Melbourne Australia

textclassics.com.au
textpublishing.com.au

The Text Publishing Company
Swann House
22 William Street
Melbourne Victoria 3000
Australia

First published by Oxford University Press, London, 1960
This edition published by The Text Publishing Company 2013

Cover design by WH Chong
Page design by Text
Typeset by Midland Typesetting

Printed in Australia by Griffin Press, an Accredited ISO AS/NZS 14001:2004 Environmental Management System printer

Primary print ISBN: 9781922147172
Ebook ISBN: 9781922148247
Author: Spence, Eleanor, 1928-2008 author.
Title: Lillipilly Hill / by Eleanor Spence; introduced by Ursula Dubosarsky.
Series: Text classics.
Subjects: Country life—Australia—Juvenile fiction.
Dewey Number: A823.3

This book is printed on paper certified against the Forest Stewardship Council® Standards. Griffin Press holds FSC chain-of-custody certification SGS-COC-005088. FSC promotes environmentally responsible, socially beneficial and economically viable management of the world's forests.

CONTENTS

Something Shining
by Ursula Dubosarsky

ELEANOR Spence always knew she was going to be a writer, but as she grew into adulthood it did not occur to her that she would write for children. How could it? A serious writer in her generation would not think of writing for children. She wrote in her 1988 memoir, *Another October Child*:

> Had anybody ever suggested that, when one day I did achieve my ambition of being a writer, I would write for and about children, I should probably have been affronted. Books for young people had no place whatsoever in the English syllabus; such a notion would have been ludicrous in the forties...There was no such thing as Children's Literature, especially in an Australian context.

Yet by the time of her death in 2008, she had produced a score of piercing, gentle, prizewinning novels for and about children, which formed a vital contribution to the creation of the body of work that became modern Australian children's literature and established the reputation of Australian children's books internationally. How did it happen?

Born Eleanor Kelly in 1928, she grew up in the Erina district of the Central Coast of New South Wales. Her father was an Australian returned serviceman and orchard farmer and her mother a Scottish high-school teacher.

Life on the Central Coast in the 1930s was secluded, almost hidden. Observant, sensitive and fervently attached to her mother, Spence was a self-confessed romantic child, who wanted the world to be full of beautiful loving and loveable things but was afraid that it might not be. Her mother was determined to give her three children the gift of a happy childhood, because she had not had one herself, and she succeeded—at least in the daytime. At night, alone in the darkness, Eleanor suffered extreme terrors. Her greatest remembered horror was the sound of a horseman galloping down the street outside—'...the approach of a single horse at night, with no certain knowledge of the rider's identity,' would resound all her life.

But the daylight was full to the brim with simple and sincere pleasures—Shirley Temple, Snow White, George MacDonald, swimming, biking, hiking, picnics and fancy dress balls. Eleanor moved happily through primary school to matriculation from Gosford High. Even the undeniable facts of World War II and the death of a close friend could not truly undermine daytime Eleanor's belief in a good world. Then she enrolled in an Arts degree at Sydney University, leaving home to live in the Country Women's Association hostel in Kings Cross. The change and social isolation was a shock. She wrote in 1980:

> All the harsher realities of life, the conflicts
> and personality problems and successes and
> failures, waited ahead in our adolescence,
> and I may have been less ready than others
> to come to grips with them. That is another
> country again, where the dreams change.

Yet cope she did, slowly making friends, conducting romances and eventually passing her exams. All the time her chief ambition was to be a writer, although she struggled to find what she wanted to write. Eleanor graduated in 1949, and after a disappointing year teaching in a girls boarding school, she undertook a librarianship course at the State Library of New South Wales. This led to work in Canberra where she met

John Spence. They married in 1952 and, along with many others of their generation, took a boat together to the UK.

It was there that it happened. Finding work as a librarian in the city of Coventry, Spence was handed the task of choosing books for the children's collection. She was obliged to read an enormous number of children's novels, good and bad, and was confronted with the rich, creative possibilities of the genre. She was also particularly struck by the lack of books about Australian children—it was as though Australia scarcely existed. She decided that she would try to write one herself, and in doing so discovered the aesthetic form that most suited her sensibilities as a writer and what she wanted to say.

Back in Australia, now with a young family, Spence took to writing at night when everyone was asleep. The fictional children that emerged from her mind were so vivid they seemed, she said, 'almost as real as my own'. She submitted her first novel to Frank Eyre at the Australian office of Oxford University Press, who was developing a list for Australian children. And so her career began.

Lillipilly Hill, published in 1960, is her third novel. It is set in a fictionalised version of the Erina district of Spence's childhood, around 1875–80. While it could be described as a historical novel, it is essentially a family story with a historical setting. It displays all the qualities that marked Spence's later, more celebrated work—the melodic language, the strength of character and theme, and the intense sympathy for the child's point of view.

The prime mover of the story is twelve-year-old Harriet, the middle child of a newly arrived family from London. Harriet is the imaginative codebreaker and the challenger of her parents' British preconceptions as they discover their new country. Her first triumph is to convince her parents to let her go to the local public school, rather than be privately educated by a governess:

> 'But why should we be different?' burst out Harriet. 'Why can't we go to the same school as these other children? We live here too, in the middle of the bush, just like them.'

In this Harriet prevails, and the three children are enrolled at the local one-teacher school along with everyone else. But not all of Harriet's attempted inversions of the social order succeed. Both Harriet and the novel continually ask the big questions: What is education for? What makes a boy a boy and a girl a girl? What is Australia? Perhaps above all, what is freedom? Harriet's family have land, education, class. But Harriet envies the personal freedom of her working-class friend Dinny O'Brien, who can climb trees, go barefoot and take off by herself to the seaside whenever she wants. Yet Harriet knows that Dinny is destined for a lifetime of impoverished housekeeping.

Nor does Harriet have the freedom of her brother, Aidan, who will be sent to Sydney Grammar to prepare him for university, while Harriet and her sister will stay at home learning dancing, piano and how to wear nice clothes, none of which Harriet can bear. Still, Aidan too is trapped—he is not a 'boy' as the schoolchildren of Lillipilly Hill understand a boy to be. He's an intellectual and is labelled a coward because he doesn't want to fight in the playground. Running away one night in misery, he befriends another boy, Clay, son of an English father and Aboriginal mother. Clay lives in a cave with his dog. He is a kind of Huck Finn character, a boy who answers to nobody, and the children are in awe of his freedom and independence. But what kind of society is it, if a boy like Clay can only feel the freedom to be himself alone in a cave?

Spence reminds the reader that the world is not easy, but that this is the world we are in and the world we must somehow come to terms with. Or try to change it, as Harriet does, with some failures along the way.

In her later work, Spence turned to urban settings, and stories about identity, religious bigotry, class, gender, autism, homosexuality. But however complex or controversial the issues, she wrote about them as children understand them, which is often largely implicitly. Spence said of herself, 'I cannot recall any point in time when I ceased once and for all to be a child, or another when I suddenly turned into an adult.' This is perhaps her greatest gift: to truly remember, and then to evoke, the child's point of view.

For Spence, leaving childhood was experienced as an acute loss—not a loss of innocence exactly, but a loss of brave intensity, of something shining. She was cynical about the triumphant progress to maturity, saying that 'it seems to me that by supressing the child in ourselves, we run the risk of denying the best part of us'. In this gentle, emotional novel of an Australian rural childhood, Spence has captured a enduring vision of that brightness, that 'best part'.

Lillipilly Hill

1

Problems and Plans

Holding their breath, the children listened for the splash.

'There they go!'

It was a good, satisfying splash. The creek water was high after the February rain, and the Wilmot buggy was heavy, and well loaded with Miss Oliver's luggage. The children were silent until the clip-clop of Barrel's hooves, and the rolling of the wheels, were no more than faint echoes in the gully, dying away along the Blackhill road.

'So that's that,' said Harriet. 'We won't see her again.'

Rose-Ann sniffled.

'You shouldn't sound so pleased, Harriet. She's been our governess for four whole years, and you liked her—you said you did.'

Harriet continued to smile, and to swing her long, black-booted legs as she sat on the top bar of the gate.

'I know. But think of no more lessons, at least for a few weeks. Father says it will be frightfully hard to find a new governess here. He'll have to go to Sydney to look for one.'

'Will he take us with him?' asked Rose-Ann hopefully.

'Of course not. It's nearly a day's journey, and it would cost too much to take us.'

They were quiet again for a few minutes. Rose-Ann was thinking wistfully of Sydney, and the shops, and the omnibuses, and the steamers on the Harbour. She could not understand why her father had not stayed there, instead of bringing them all on to this strange place after only three days of Sydney's delights.

Harriet stared down through the trees at the half-seen water of the creek, glinting fiercely where the hot sun touched it.

'You know,' she said, with unusual seriousness, 'I do think Miss Oliver might have stayed longer. We've only been here a month. How can you get to know a place properly in a month?'

4

Aidan spoke for the first time, putting aside his book. He was sprawled in the shade at the bottom of the gate, disliking the sunlight as intensely as Harriet rejoiced in it.

'She knew it well enough to know she could never live here. You can't blame her, can you?'

'No,' said Rose-Ann, looking mournful again. 'I don't want to live here, either. Nobody would.'

'Oh, don't be silly,' said Harriet impatiently. 'A whole month, and we've never been farther than the bottom of the hill! Do you know *anything* about this place? Why! I'm sure neither of you even know what it's called.'

Aidan and Rose-Ann gave her identical glances of pained surprise.

'Of course we do,' said Aidan. 'The property is called Mount Agnes. It was named for Uncle John's wife.'

'That's just its Sunday name,' said Harriet scornfully. 'Do you know what everyone calls it? Lillipilly Hill. And I can tell you why, too.'

Aidan, annoyed by his young sister's air of triumph, was none the less interested. Rose-Ann merely looked bewildered.

'What a funny name! I don't like it at all.'

'It's because of these trees,' said Harriet, gesturing to right and left.

Aidan stared at them, really seeing them for the first time. There were two, one on either side of the wooden gate. They were big enough to climb, with straight, greyish trunks and a tangle of branches clothed in stiff, shiny, green leaves. At present they bore round, wine-red berries, many of which had fallen and lay crushed beneath the children's boots.

'I've never seen trees like that before,' he admitted. 'I suppose they're called lillipillies, are they?'

'Yes, they are. And these two have been here since Uncle John built the house,' explained Harriet. 'So the people living in the village called it Lillipilly Hill. Boz told me.'

'Boz?' repeated Aidan in surprise. 'But he never talks, unless sometimes to Polly.'

'He talks to *me*,' said Harriet proudly. 'I just keep on asking questions. I go down to the cowshed at milking time, and then he can't run away.'

'But you aren't allowed to play down there,' protested Rose-Ann. 'And it's a barn, anyway.'

'It is not,' retorted Harriet. 'It's never called a barn here. That's just what I mean—you two don't know *anything*.'

'Rose-Ann mightn't know very much,' said Aidan with dignity. 'She's only ten, and she doesn't keep on asking so many questions that people's heads start to buzz—like you, Harriet. But I know a great deal about Uncle John, and how the convicts built the house, and how he left it to Father because Father was his favourite nephew. Father told me all about it, months ago, before we even sailed.'

'That's all like a history lesson,' said Harriet. 'We have to find out what Lillipilly Hill is like *now*.'

'I think you've been out in the sun too long,' said Aidan unkindly. 'Where's your sun-bonnet?'

Almost at once, his question was echoed from the house.

'Harriet, where's your sun-bonnet? Put it on immediately!'

Harriet jumped off the gate on to the garden path, and snatched the hated white bonnet off a straggling rosebush. Aidan's commands could comfortably be ignored, but not those of her father, who stood now on the wide, stone-flagged veranda, wrinkling his face against the glare from outdoors.

'Come inside, children. Your mother and I want to talk to you.'

'What's happened?' whispered Aidan, rising and brushing grass-seeds from his jacket. 'What have you been doing, Harriet?'

'Nothing,' answered Harriet indignantly. 'Why should it always be me?'

Aidan glanced at his two sisters. As usual, they were dressed alike in gingham dresses and holland pinafores, but there all resemblance ceased. Rose-Ann's spotless bonnet was set squarely on shining fair curls, while Harriet's had been tossed anyhow on top of her dishevelled mop of sandy hair. Rose-Ann's skin was as smooth and pale as when she had left London four months ago, while Harriet's thin, pointed face was red with sunburn, and already beginning to freckle. Her pinafore was stained with blackberry juice, and one bootlace was undone.

'Your looking-glass will tell you why,' said Aidan, leading the way towards the house.

Harriet glared at the rose-bushes, seeing only the devouring weeds and overgrown branches where once Great-Aunt Agnes had enjoyed beauty and order. More than a year had passed since John Wilmot's death, and Boz, the caretaker, had had little time to spare for gardening. Beyond the rose-garden, the lovingly-planted English shrubs were engulfed in a sea of lucerne, and a fine variety of weeds with unknown names. Only the hardy geraniums bloomed still along the edge of the veranda, and a blue convolvulus climbed one of the hardwood posts.

Francis Wilmot watched his children come down the path in the brilliant sunlight.

'We are having a cup of tea in the sitting-room,' he said. 'Polly has put out milk and cake for you.'

Agreeably surprised at such refreshment in the middle of the morning, the children entered the broad hall which cut the house in half. The polished cedar floor and the unpapered wooden walls gave a feeling of coolness, and made the hall so dark that the children blinked, momentarily blinded. The sitting-room was at the front of the house, with shuttered french windows opening on to the veranda. It was a square, solid room, furnished with the handsome, heavy, much-polished pieces that Aunt Agnes had brought with her from her old home in London. Its neat, rather sombre air was in startling contrast to the bright untidiness glimpsed through the western windows.

Mrs Wilmot drew Rose-Ann and Harriet down beside her on the sofa. She looked cool and immaculate in a lilac-coloured dress with a little high, white collar. Side by side, she and Rose-Ann were pleasingly alike, just as Aidan and his father, facing each other across the massive stone fireplace, appeared to be cut to an identical pattern.

'I just don't look as if I belonged to this family,' reflected Harriet. It was an interesting thought—if she was not a Wilmot, then who was she? A lost princess, perhaps? Or a daughter of the wilds, like Lorna Doone?

She caught sight of the cake-stand, and for the time being, at least, was content to be a Wilmot. It was a currant cake. Polly had a light hand with most kinds of cake, but currant cakes were really her masterpieces. Harriet took a large slice—one of her mother's complaints about Polly was that she would never learn elegance in her serving of food. Harriet had no such fault to find.

'I expect you were very sorry to see Miss Oliver go,' sighed Mrs Wilmot. 'She felt so badly about parting from you after all this time.'

Rose-Ann made noises of agreement, and Harriet started to wriggle.

'If we get a new governess, Father, what about me?' asked Aidan. 'I'm too old for governesses now.'

Mr Wilmot frowned into his tea-cup.

'Of course you are. I'm only too well aware of it. You're part of the whole problem.'

'What problem?' demanded Harriet, confident now that she was not to be rebuked for any wrong-doing. Her visits to the cowshed had apparently not been discovered.

'The problem, Harriet, is one of money—to put it briefly.'

The children, surprised at being taken thus into adult confidence, gazed at their father inquiringly.

'You see, I don't think we can afford a new governess, still less a tutor for Aidan,' explained Mr Wilmot. 'I thought it best for you to know all this—you are no longer in the nursery. And what I am about to decide will affect the future of all of you.'

'No governess and no tutor,' murmured Aidan. 'That only leaves school.'

'For all of us?' asked Harriet eagerly.

'I'm afraid school is out of the question too—it would have to be boarding-school, you see. Your mother and I simply did not understand, when we agreed to leave home and take up farming here as Uncle John wished, just how difficult it would be to live in a civilized fashion. The property yields very little income—Uncle John was a far wealthier man than I. If we stayed here, it would be impossible for you children to have the education we want you to have. It would also mean that your mother had to work far too hard to keep the house in order, without suitable help. And you would all be condemned to live cut off from the kind of society to which you have been accustomed. In short, I think that I must sell the property and take you all home.'

Home—Harriet shut her eyes and tried to remember what the word meant. A tall, blank-faced, sedate old house in a quiet Kensington square. Walks

in the Gardens in autumn, just before they sailed—
the trees all brown and gold, and the sun dusky pink
through the mist. Fires in the schoolroom, and muffins
for tea. The jogging and rattling of tradesmen's vans
in the square, and the brisk tip-tap of her father's
feet as he returned from his mysterious work in the
City—mysterious because it had never been explained
to Harriet, the only one who sometimes wondered
where the money came from to buy her clothes and
pay for dancing lessons and pantomimes.

She opened her eyes, and looked out through the
door. The sun, nearing its peak, still poured its relentless
heat on the tangled garden. But beneath the willow near
the side fence, the grass seemed cool and inviting, and
beyond the willow and the rocky hill-side lay a whole
new world that Harriet had hardly begun to know.
Surely 'home' was the place where one liked to live?

'And then would I go to Rugby, after all?' asked
Aidan.

'Perhaps. We would have to wait and see.' There
was a trace of disappointment in Mr Wilmot's voice.
He was proud of his son's cleverness, his studious
habits, his steady ambition—but now he wanted to
find something more than that. Yet how could he
expect the boy to understand his father's feelings about
Mount Agnes? Aidan would merely be puzzled to learn

12

that to Francis Wilmot, giving up his uncle's property meant the end of a lifelong dream. And that the prospect of returning to book-keeping in the Wilmot family firm was like a vision of slavery.

'And I could go back to Mrs Christie's dancing-class,' said Rose-Ann with satisfaction. 'And wear my party dress again.'

'"One-two-three, one-two-three, *do* try harder, Harriet, dear",' Harriet muttered, savagely mimicking Mrs Christie's ladylike voice.

'Harriet, you must leave the room if you're going to be rude,' said her mother sternly. 'Mrs Christie tried very hard to make you into a young lady with pretty manners, which is what we want you to be. That is why your father is prepared to take you home to London.'

'Why can't I be a young lady here?' protested Harriet.

'How would you ever learn? The nearest school for young ladies is in Blackhill, eight miles away—how would you reach it? You can be sure that we have thought of every possibility. And I, for one, will be very pleased when we are all settled at home again. So do try and be a help, Harriet.'

Harriet lapsed into glum silence. She thought she caught a gleam of sympathy in her father's expression, but she wasn't sure.

'I don't think there's much more to be said,' Mr Wilmot concluded, standing up. 'I shall go to Blackhill tomorrow and begin arrangements for the sale of the property.'

Dismissed, the children returned to the garden. But Harriet discovered suddenly that she did not want to talk to the others about her father's announcement, and set off instead towards the cowshed.

This time she went by a lengthy and indirect route, in order to avoid passing the windows of the sitting-room, where her father and mother were still talking. She followed the veranda around to the eastern side, past the bedrooms. If the front garden could be called untidy, then the eastern part of the grounds was almost a jungle. A brilliantly purple bougainvillea vine had draped itself over the veranda posts and even invaded the guttering, casting deep shade over the stone flags of the veranda. Near by a struggling grape-vine clung to a lopsided wire trellis—Harriet plucked a few small, black grapes, and shuddered at their sourness. Somewhere among the towering lantanas by the fence was an ornamental pond, once stocked with fish, but now half-choked with weeds, and providing a fertile breeding-ground for mosquitoes.

Harriet kept to the narrow path, mindful of her mother's warnings about snakes, and pushed open the gate that led to the back yard. This was really forbidden territory, but to Harriet it was the most interesting part of the property. It was the domain of Polly, the maid-of-all-work, and Boz, the cowman-labourer-gardener. On Harriet's right, a fence of wooden posts and slackened wire divided the yard from the orchard, which stretched away down the hill-side. Ahead were two tall old mulberry trees, supporting between them an overburdened clothes-line, and close by, a massive copper on a stone fire-place. The fire had long since gone out, for Polly did the washing before breakfast.

Harriet went on, past the woodpile, and the vegetable garden, and the sagging tomato plants. On her left, beneath a fig-tree, was the well, which added to the water-supply provided by the three iron tanks at the back of the house.

The cowshed was deserted. It served as a stable too, but Barrel's stall was empty, and no hard-worked Boz was busy among the cow-bails and feed-troughs.

'But of course he wouldn't be back yet,' Harriet reminded herself. 'It's nearly an hour's drive to Blackhill. Bother!'

She wandered over to the fig-tree, and climbed on to the coping of the well to pick some of the fruit. It was very strange, she reflected, as she bit through the purple skin, to think that only four weeks ago she had never tasted a fresh fig, and now they were almost her favourite fruit. Almost, but not quite, for the peaches that grew at the top of the orchard were the biggest, the sweetest, and the juiciest she had ever known. It was a great pity that they were finished.

The back yard was very quiet, and not the faintest breath of wind stirred the dark-green leaves above Harriet's head. She leant forward and gazed down into the black depths of the well, wishing she could strip off her heavy boots and stockings and go barefoot. She might even paddle in the creek. But such activities were impossible for a young English lady, no matter how oppressive the heat.

The back door was flung open, and Polly came down the steps, carrying a plate on which rested a round, golden pat of butter. She came over to the well, and bent to place the butter on a shelf in the stone, just above the water.

'The butter nearly runs away while I look at it,' she observed cheerfully. 'And I've been half the morning making it, too.'

'Why do you put it in the well?' asked Harriet.

Polly stared at her.

'Why indeed! You don't know much, do you? To keep it cool, of course.' Her voice was rough, but far from unkind. She was a plump, brisk, red-headed girl, eighteen years old—Harriet had certainly never encountered a servant quite like her. Polly 'lacked respect', Mrs Wilmot said, and could rarely bring herself to address the children as 'Miss' or 'Master'. She was a Colonial born and bred, and although she had been in domestic service for six years, she had lost none of her native toughness and independence.

She looked at Harriet now with a lively curiosity.

'So your Miss Oliver's gone and left, has she? What do you think of that?'

'I don't know,' said Harriet truthfully. 'I think she could have stayed a little longer. She said this place was much too wild and lonely. But you like it, don't you, Polly?'

'Nothing lonely about this,' declared Polly. 'This is the best place I've ever been in. Only five of you to cook and wash and clean for—I had ten in my last sittywation! Had to get up at five, and went to bed at ten, and never off my feet all day.'

She was only too ready for a chat. Harriet abandoned her idea of waiting for Boz, and turned to Polly instead.

'Polly, is there a school in the village?'

'The village?' repeated Polly. 'You mean Barley Creek, I suppose.'

'I mean the place down there,' said Harriet, impatiently waving her arm towards the creek.

'That's Barley Creek—we don't call it a village. Not that it's a big town, like Blackhill, but it's got a post office, and Mrs Tolly's store, and the church—'

'But has it got a *school*?' demanded Harriet.

'Indeed it has,' said Polly proudly, having already adopted Barley Creek as her native town. '*And* a school-teacher—a real one, too. Not like Winneroo—they've only got a teacher three days a week, and over at Deacon's Flat they haven't even got a school. Ours is very good, they say—not that I know much about schools. Never went to one, myself.'

Harriet gazed past the cowshed at the tall scrub which clothed the western hill-side. Somewhere down there lay the tiny township which she had not yet seen, and which she must soon explore.

'What is the school-teacher's name, and where does she live?'

'It's not a lady at all—a real gentleman, I've heard, called Mr Burnie, and he lives next to the school. It's just over the road from the post office.'

'Don't tell Mother or Father, or anyone, what I've asked you, will you? Please, Polly,' begged Harriet earnestly.

'Of course not. Why should I?' said Polly, though consumed with curiosity. 'I must go and start the bread. Did you have some of my cake?'

'Oh, yes!' Harriet searched for just the right word. 'It was most *delectable*!'

Polly gazed at her admiringly.

'My, that's a big word! I'll see you get some more cake for your tea tonight.'

She returned to the kitchen, singing lustily, and Harriet made her way back to the front garden. Aidan was still reading, and Rose-Ann was gathering flower petals, to be pressed in her biggest book.

'Come and help me, Harriet,' she called. 'I can't reach the tallest ones.'

Harriet found the occupation rather dull, but at least it gave her an opportunity to do some quiet thinking.

'Today's Friday, isn't it?' she asked, standing on tiptoe to pluck a shining yellow rose.

'Yes—only all the days are the same here,' said Rose-Ann. 'Does it matter that it's Friday?'

'Yes, it does,' answered Harriet, and was silent.

It must be nearly twelve o'clock already, and soon they would be called for the midday meal, which Mrs Wilmot termed 'luncheon', and Polly obstinately referred to as 'dinner'. After the meal the girls were expected to rest for an hour or so, and then take a short walk.

'But Miss Oliver's gone, so perhaps we'll be allowed to go for a walk with just Aidan,' Harriet said to herself. What she planned to do must be done this afternoon—tomorrow would be too late. And it was all very important. Indeed, as she went into the house to wash her hands for luncheon, she felt quite awed by the responsibility she had given herself.

2

Harriet goes Visiting

The girls' bedroom opened on to the eastern veranda.
The vines outside made it a cool, dark room, at least in
mid-afternoon. Harriet lay on her low wooden bed and
stared at the screen of bougainvillea. There was little
enough to look at in the bedroom itself—another bed,
just like her own, a washstand made of packing-cases, a
straight-backed, uninviting chair, and a gloomy picture
of a storm in some unidentified range of mountains.

'Why don't we unpack our pretty cushions and
covers and things?' grumbled Harriet.

'Mother doesn't think it would be worth while,
that's why,' said Rose-Ann. 'We mightn't be here
much longer.'

'I do think we could make our room look nicer, though,' protested Harriet. 'And I'd like a shelf for my books. Aidan has one.'

'Aidan's a boy,' said Rose-Ann logically.

Harriet sighed. That was the answer to everything. Aidan was a boy, so he had bookshelves, and a room to himself, and time to read as much as he wanted. But Harriet was always being summoned from her beloved books to practise the piano, or do her embroidery, or talk to visitors. Not that they had many visitors here— indeed, she could remember none except the minister and his wife. Now they were absent in Sydney, and the church would be without a minister until their return. And going to church, Harriet reflected, would have been one way of meeting the people of Barley Creek.

'Is it time to get up yet?' she asked Rose-Ann.

'I don't know. I can't hear Mother moving around. Who's to take us for our walk?'

'We shouldn't need to be taken by anyone now,' said Harriet crossly. 'We're old enough not to get lost. Anyway, Aidan's going with us. I'm getting up.'

She tugged on her boots, and reached for her sun-bonnet. Rather sleepily, Rose-Ann did likewise. Obeying Harriet had become a habit, no longer questioned. But by the time Rose-Ann had tied her bootlaces and adjusted her bonnet to her own satisfaction, Harriet was already on the front veranda, arguing with Aidan.

'We *are* allowed to go as far as the creek, so don't be lazy. You can take your book with you if you want, but I'm going to have a long walk.'

Aidan stuffed his book into his jacket pocket, and turned towards the gate.

'All right, Miss Have-It-Your-Own-Way. I'll be pleased if you get a new governess, I can tell you.'

In single file, they walked down the dusty track. It was barely wide enough for the buggy; on either side grew a hedge of blackberry bushes, and beyond that steep piles of grey rock rose among the foreign trees, gum and wattle and turpentine. The children's passing disturbed a flock of rosellas—they flapped away over the treetops in flashes of vivid red and green, with shrill, harsh cries that made Rose-Ann jump in fright.

'The birds here are so *noisy*,' she complained. 'There was one outside our bedroom this morning that really shouted.'

'That was a kookaburra,' said Aidan. 'You see, Harriet, I do know *some* things about New South Wales.'

'Anyone would know a kookaburra,' retorted Harriet. 'And it doesn't shout, Rose-Ann—it laughs.'

They reached the ford, and stood looking at the clear, brown water sweeping across the pebbles. The sunlight slanted down through tall tree-ferns and she-oaks, and turned to molten gold a clump of wild broom on the farther bank.

Harriet drew a deep breath.

'Now, Aidan, you can sit down and read. And Rose-Ann must stay with you. She can pick wild flowers. I'm going for a walk along the creek, and I won't be back for about half an hour. And if you go home without me I'll take back that new Henty book I gave you for Christmas.'

Before Aidan and Rose-Ann had time to speak, she marched off along the bank.

'Whatever is she up to?' wondered Aidan. 'Oh, well, this is a good place to sit, anyway. Go and pick your flowers, Rosie.'

'But I don't know any of their names,' said his orderly sister. 'I'll have to ask Harriet afterwards. Do you suppose there are snakes here, Aidan?'

'I don't know—call out if you see one,' replied Aidan indolently, settling himself comfortably against a shaded rock.

Meanwhile Harriet had come to a sort of crossroads. On her left, the path along the creek continued, a mere thread of a path between the water and the scrub. At right angles to it ran a wider track, with deeply scored wheel-marks—this apparently was the route used by the Barley Creek inhabitants to reach the ford.

'It can't be very far,' thought Harriet. 'I can see smoke over there.'

She hurried along the track, feeling hot and more than a little anxious. Half an hour was not long, when she considered what she hoped to achieve.

She came upon the settlement quite suddenly, round a curve in the track. It was set in a hollow among low rocky hills—one of them, Harriet realized, led up to the western boundary of her own home. At the foot of this hill was the little church, the only building in the township to be constructed, like the Wilmots' house, of the golden-brown Blackhill stone. Near the church was the timber Rectory, flanked by twin, torch-like poplars, and down beside the track stood two iron-roofed, unpainted shacks which Harriet recognized in surprise as the post office and the store.

She turned to study the opposite side of the track. Once her father had taken them all for a holiday in a Cotswold village, and in their walks they had often passed the village school. Thus Harriet's vision of the Barley Creek school had been of a dignified establishment in weathered stone, presided over by a gentle, middle-aged lady in black, with a white lace collar.

'But this can't be it,' Harriet told herself, staring at the one-roomed building of wattle slabs and shingle roof, at the meagre pine trees, the rusty tank, and the flat, dusty playground with scarcely a blade of grass in it.

However, it was directly opposite the post office, as Polly had said. And the few children climbing through the sliprails certainly looked as if they were on their way home from school. They stared at Harriet curiously as they passed, eyeing her well-made clothes, her stout boots, and white bonnet. The one girl in the group was barefoot, and wore no bonnet or pinafore—her dress was of faded blue gingham, much too small for her.

Harriet glanced away from them, too proud to ask for directions. Mr Burnie lived next to the school, according to Polly, and there was only one house visible on that side, a windowless cottage, also of slabs, but brightened by the little well-kept garden that surrounded it.

Harriet crossed to the white paling fence. A man was digging near the gate, a small, plump man with a fair beard. His smile, when he looked up and saw Harriet, was reassuring—the most hopeful sign Harriet had seen that afternoon.

26

'Are you Mr Burnie?' she asked.

'Indeed I am. What can I do for you?' His voice was English and pleasant.

'I've only got half an hour, and it's not really long enough,' said Harriet breathlessly. 'I want to ask you about your school.'

'Bless you, it's not mine,' said Mr Burnie cheerfully. 'It belongs to the worthy Department of Public Instruction. I just rent it, so to speak. Won't you come in? Mrs Burnie has just made a pot of tea.'

'Thank you,' said Harriet, 'but what I want to ask is a secret, you see.'

'Mrs Burnie keeps secrets very well,' the schoolteacher said. 'However, if you wish, we shall take our tea on the veranda, which will be quite private.'

In a remarkably short space of time Harriet was seated in a shabby old rocking-chair, behind a lattice hung with roses, while Mr Burnie handed her tea and cake. It was much cooler here, for a gentle nor'easter had crept up during the afternoon, and Harriet's spirits, never low for long, began to return to their usual level.

'I don't believe we have met,' said Mr Burnie, sitting down on the front step. 'Certainly you aren't one of my pupils.'

'I'm Harriet Wilmot,' explained Harriet. 'We live up there—on the hill. We only came four weeks ago.'

27

Mr Burnie looked at her with greater interest.

'Of course—then it must have been your great-uncle who built the house. The district is very proud of him, I believe. I came here just after he died.'

Harriet rapidly told the story of Uncle John's legacy, and her father's decision to accept it.

'But now, you see,' she concluded sadly, 'there's not much money left, and our governess wouldn't stay, and Mother thinks this is no place for young ladies to grow up in. Only I don't want to be a young lady, and I like living here, though the others don't.'

'It sounds very difficult,' agreed Mr Burnie. 'And how do you think my school could help you?'

'This is the hard part,' said Harriet, carefully putting down her tea-cup. 'I wanted to ask you to call on Father.'

Mr Burnie looked puzzled.

'I shall, certainly, but what am I to say to him?'

Harriet nearly upset the rocking-chair in her eagerness.

'Tell him—*please* tell him—that you have a school here, and that you could take my brother and sister and me, and teach us everything we would learn at home. And then Father wouldn't have to worry about us not being properly educated—especially Aidan, because he's a boy.'

'Well now, Miss Harriet, I think I see what you mean,' said the schoolmaster, placidly filling his pipe. 'But it's not altogether as simple as that. To begin with—have you seen the school?'

'Only the outside,' said Harriet, staring in sudden gloom at the crimson roses.

'Inside, it's no better. We have been promised a new building, but no one knows when we shall have it. It's hardly the sort of school you would attend in London, is it? I have twenty-one pupils, the oldest thirteen and the youngest four. They are quite agreeable children, but I don't think your parents would have chosen them to be your companions. And by no means could my school be called an establishment for young ladies.'

'But why should we be different?' burst out Harriet. 'Why can't we go to the same school as these other children? We live here too, in the middle of the bush, just like them.'

'You say you won't be living here for long,' Mr Burnie reminded her gently. 'Doesn't that show that your father and mother want something better for you? But tell me about your brother and sister, and yourself, and I promise to do what I can.'

'Aidan's the important one,' said Harriet, with a sigh. 'He's thirteen, and very clever. Everyone says so. He reads and reads—not story books, like me, but history and all about Ancient Greece and Rome, and stories of explorers and inventors and people. He wants to be a lawyer. He would have been sent to Rugby next year if we had stayed at home, and he was always at the top of his form at his prep. school. Rose-Ann is ten. She's not clever, but she's pretty, and she can sew and do embroidery, and she was the best in our dancing-class. She likes those things, you see.'

'And you?' prompted Mr Burnie.

'Oh, I'm the middle one. I had my birthday on the ship, on the way out to Sydney. I'm twelve. I hate sewing and dancing, but I do like reading. I can't quite decide which is my favourite story—*Lorna Doone* or *At the Back of the North Wind*. I've read them both four times.'

'They're very different, aren't they? Remind me to lend you a new story—it's called *Treasure Island*, and I feel sure you will need to hide it from your brother if you want to keep it. But to return to your problems— I think Aidan will be easiest of all to teach. I could tutor him for a scholarship to the Sydney Grammar School, which is an excellent establishment. I already have one scholarship pupil—Charles Farmer, the minister's boy. He's the same age as your brother. I would explain all this to your father in detail, of course.'

He paused, puffing at his pipe, and watching the shadows stretch over the garden. Harriet had an uneasy feeling that it must be quite late.

'What about Rose-Ann and me? At home we learnt things like writing and spelling and history and geography, and we had music lessons and sewing as well.'

'If your father and mother ever consented to your attending this school—which, I am afraid, I rather doubt—you would certainly learn how to spell and write and all the rest of it, but I would never venture to give lessons in music or any other such extra. There are no dancing-classes even in Blackhill. How could you hope to find them in Barley Creek?'

Harriet rose, and tied on her sun-bonnet.

'Thank you very much, Mr Burnie, and I'm sure Father will be pleased to see you. And would you be able to call tonight, as he will be going to Blackhill early tomorrow, to arrange about the sale of the house?'

Mr Burnie laughed.

'You are still quite hopeful, then? I promise I shall do my very best for you. Good luck, Harriet.'

Harriet marched off down the path, head held high, refusing to recognize the fact that the schoolmaster regarded her quest as more than a little forlorn. She was so busy with her own thoughts that

Mr Burnie had to call after her twice before she heard him.

'Your book, Harriet—you've forgotten it.'

Once out of the gate, with *Treasure Island* tucked safely under her arm, Harriet began to run. She sped past the schoolhouse, pulling a face at it as she went, past the post office and store and church, disregarding the stares of one or two startled townsfolk, and found the track along the creek. Her noisy progress put to flight a dozen unseen creatures in the bush beside her—lizards and snakes and bandicoots, and the ugly, leathery goannas basking on the sunny rocks. Harriet heard nothing but the thudding of her boots in the dust, and saw only the tunnel of trees ahead.

Aidan sat exactly where she had left him, but of Rose-Ann there was no sign. Aidan greeted his sister with a frown.

'Wherever have you been? Rose-Ann went home— she said she was frightened of snakes. I took her as far as the front gate, so I expect no one will worry.'

'I didn't mean to be so long,' panted Harriet. 'But I've got lots to tell you.'

'No time now,' said Aidan, rising. 'After tea will do. Where did you get that book?'

'It was lent to me by a friend,' replied Harriet loftily. 'I might let you read it when I've finished.'

After her long run from the township, and a rapid scramble up the hill with Aidan, Harriet was too breathless to eat her tea. She sat hunched over the cedar table in the dining-room, a dark slit of a room next to the kitchen, and gazed without enthusiasm at the bread and butter and the tall jug of milk.

'Polly said we were to have currant cake,' she protested.

'Mother said no cake if we were late home from our walk,' said Rose-Ann. 'And you and Aidan *were* late. So I didn't get any cake either.'

'I'll ask Polly to give you some afterwards,' promised Harriet. 'And really Aidan ought to have some too, because it wasn't his fault.'

'I don't mind,' said Aidan generously. 'But you must tell us what you were doing this afternoon.'

'I can't tell you here,' said Harriet mysteriously. 'It's very, very private. Let's go down to the Ruins after tea, and I'll tell you there.'

It was half past five when the children climbed through the sliprail into the orchard, and followed the path between the rows of trees, apple and peach and apricot, which spread down the eastern slope of Lillipilly Hill. Half-way down Harriet led the procession off to the right, for the Ruins had been her discovery, and were almost her own property. No one else but

33

the children visited the tumbledown, weed-choked remains of the stone huts which Uncle John had built to house his convict labourers, fifty years ago.

'We'll go round to the back,' decided Harriet. 'There are some good stones there to sit on, and no one can see us.'

Certainly they could feel quite alone here, perched among the blackberries, with the fading sunlight on their backs. Before them lay no faintest sign of human habitation, beyond the wire fence of the orchard. Grey-green hills rolled on into blue distance, ending in the darker line that was the sea. Far to the right, light gleamed on the long inlet known as Black-hill Bay, whence the steam packets sailed daily for Sydney, fifty miles to the south.

'Miss Oliver will be in Sydney now,' said Rose-Ann wistfully. 'She leaves for London on Monday.'

'There's no use your wanting to go back home, Rose-Ann,' said Harriet positively. 'We're not going.'

Aidan stopped slapping at mosquitoes to stare at her.

'How do you know? Did Father tell you?'

'No,' said Harriet grandly. 'It's all my idea. I've thought of a way to get us all properly taught, so we won't have to go back to London to school. I don't want to go, and I don't believe Father does, either.'

34

'But *we* want to go,' cried Rose-Ann. 'Mother and Aidan and me.'

'It's all very well for you, Harriet,' said Aidan, with that cold condescension which his sister greatly disliked. 'You're just a girl, with no career to think about. You like it here, because you can do all sorts of things you wouldn't be allowed to do at home. But I want to go to a good school, and then to study law. How can I do that here?'

'I know a way,' said Harriet stubbornly. 'I've met the schoolmaster, and he says he will tutor you for a scholarship to the Sydney Grammar School. I'm sure he's just as good a master as the ones at home.'

'You mean you went to see him, all by yourself?' gasped Rose-Ann.

'Yes, this afternoon. His name's Mr Burnie, and he's coming to see Father tonight, to tell him all about the school, and scholarships, and things.'

She could see that Aidan was impressed, although he would not admit it. If she could win Aidan over to her side, then the battle would be half-won already. Rose-Ann's opposition was not likely to be very strong.

'And would we go to this school, too?' asked Rose-Ann.

'I don't know yet,' said Harriet. 'Mother will have to decide. But I want you to ask if we can go, Rose-

Ann—Mother might agree if we both seem pleased about it.'

'But I'm not pleased a bit!' wailed Rose-Ann. 'I've never been to a school at all, and we don't know anything about this one.'

Harriet leant forward so that her face almost touched her sister's, and lowered her voice.

'Just think, Rose-Ann, if we have to go home, you'll have to stay on that ship again, and it will be even worse than last time, because you won't have Miss Oliver to look after you!'

Rose-Ann stared in horror at Harriet's intent and unrelenting face. The memory of the voyage out to Sydney was still all too clear in Rose-Ann's mind— thirteen weeks of seasick, homesick, bewildered misery, divided between pitching decks and stuffy, overcrowded cabin. Rose-Ann was fond of comfort of all kinds, and her spirit quailed at the thought of another sea voyage so soon. Even her beloved dancing-classes could not make up for it.

'Stop frightening her,' ordered Aidan. 'You're just trying to make her do what you want, Harriet. It's not fair.'

'It is! You're the ones that aren't being fair!' cried Harriet. 'You want to run away from here just because you can't have the same things that you'd have at home! You like reading about explorers, Aidan, but you could never be one yourself—you wouldn't dare. You're *afraid* of this place!'

Aidan rarely lost his temper. He simply went his own quiet, leisurely way, treating others with cool aloofness when they annoyed him. But now his pale, clever face was red with anger.

'That's not true! And I'll prove it! I'll go to your wretched little school, and I'll work harder than anyone, and I'll get that scholarship. But don't ask me to like it, and I don't feel like speaking to you ever again.'

He hurried away through the darkening orchard, his footsteps breaking into the twilight chorus of crickets and frogs.

'Now we won't see him for days,' said Rose-Ann tearfully. 'Oh, I wish we'd all stayed at home! *Why* do you want us to live here, Harriet?'

Harriet looked up through the fruit trees towards the house. At the crest of the hill, just behind the cowshed, grew three huge old bluegums, black now against a pink and gold sky.

'One day I'm going to climb those trees,' said Harriet. 'And I'm going to fish in the creek, and explore in the bush, and talk to all those people down there. I never knew there were so many lovely things to do. I'm not going to call London "home" any more.'

Rose-Ann sighed, and scratched a mosquito bite. When Harriet talked like that, it was useless to try and argue with her.

'Come on,' said Rose-Ann. 'Polly will be lighting the lamps.'

3

On Trial

Harriet was dreaming that she was on board ship, sailing on and on over an endless, fiery sea, beneath a burning red sky. Aidan was shut up in the cabin, and was tapping on the door, but Harriet, held fast in the awful immobility of dreams, could not go to him.

She woke, and the tapping went on. It was a peewit, knocking his beak against the window-pane, and staring fixedly at Harriet with impudent, beady eyes.

Harriet sat up.

'No wonder I was hot in my dream,' she thought. 'It's like an oven in here.'

The rising sun had poked its long fingers through the vines and across the veranda and into the bedroom.

Harriet jumped out of bed and pattered over the bare, wooden floor. She was wearing a pink flannel nightgown—it was much too warm for flannel, but Mrs Wilmot mistrusted the night air, which, she felt, ought to be cool.

Rose-Ann was still asleep, looking as neat and pretty as when she was awake. The sunlight turned her hair into threads of gold, and strayed over her flushed face, but she did not stir.

Harriet went out on to the veranda. The peewit hopped away across the stone flags, and she followed, rejoicing in the coolness beneath her feet. She was about to coax the peewit on to her hand when a voice called: 'Harriet!'

She had not expected to see her father up and about so early. He stood at the corner of the veranda, fully dressed—but not, she noticed at once, in his town-going clothes.

'Go and get dressed, Harriet, and then we'll take a short walk. I want to talk to you. Don't forget to brush your hair.'

The tone of his voice told her nothing. She scurried back into the bedroom, and scrambled into her clothes as rapidly as she could. She was still accustomed to having Miss Oliver help her with tapes and ribbons, but she managed everything to her own satisfaction, except for the fixing of a semi-circular comb in her unruly hair. Eventually she threw down the comb in disgust, tugged on her sun-bonnet, and ran to join her father.

'Where are we going?' she asked. She was not at all sure of her father's mood—was he angry with her over Mr Burnie's visit? It would not be surprising if he were, she reflected dismally. Fathers did not expect their twelve-year-old daughters to arrange affairs for them. And he must know now that she had gone down to Barley Creek alone, which could be regarded as deceitful, to say the least.

'Where would you like to go?' said Mr Wilmot. 'It's such a beautiful morning for walking.'

'We could go down to the bottom of the orchard,' suggested Harriet. 'And come back round the front garden.'

'Very well,' agreed her father, and they set off past the grape-vines to the sliprail.

Harriet walked with unusual decorum, keeping to the path, and not once breaking into a run or a skip. Ahead, her father's tall, straight figure moved between the graceful trees, now and then brushing a spider's web that stretched glistening from branch to branch. A few cicadas were tuning up for the day—Harriet glanced eagerly about her, trying to see them, but the green and yellow and black shapes were well hidden. It was far easier to see the active little grey-green silver-eyes, busily raiding the fruit trees.

'You seem to know the property well, Harriet,' said Mr Wilmot, pausing to pick a ripening apple. 'I gather you like being here?'

'Yes,' muttered Harriet.

Her father turned to look at her.

'So much, in fact, that you asked the schoolmaster to take all three of you as his pupils?'

Harriet gazed at a particularly bold silver-eye pecking at an apple a few feet away.

'I didn't say that exactly—'

'Mr Burnie was here last night. He told me what you had asked him. I must say, Harriet, you take rather a lot upon yourself. Your mother was horrified.'

This being the type of grown-up remark to which there was obviously no answer, Harriet continued to stare silently at the birds.

'Let us finish our walk,' suggested her father.

They went on past the track that led to the Ruins, and came at last to the orchard fence.

'I've never seen a view quite like this,' said Mr Wilmot. 'So completely untouched.'

They gazed together at the sun-tipped hills, the glistening sea, and the cloudless, bright sky. The clear chime of a bell-bird came from the gully beneath them, followed by the long-drawn cry of a coachwhip.

'I don't wonder that you want to stay, Harriet,' said Mr Wilmot. 'I want to stay, myself. But we must think of the others. I like Mr Burnie, and I believe his plans for Aidan might prove quite sound. As for you and Rose-Ann—'

He broke off to listen to an early-morning chorus of kookaburras, lined up on the topmost branch of a redgum beyond the fence.

'Wonderful noise, isn't it? We have agreed, Mr Burnie and your mother and I, that you girls will attend the school every morning, and that in the afternoon you will go to Mrs Burnie for sewing, or, we hope, to Mrs Farmer for music lessons. The rest of the afternoons will be spent with your mother.'

This was far better than Harriet had dared to hope. She hopped from foot to foot with excitement.

'Then we will stay?'

'For the time being. We have decided to give it six months' trial. Whether we remain after that depends on many things—how well I can work the farm, how your mother's health keeps in this new climate, and, above all, how much help you children can give her. I mean help of all kinds.'

'Like making our own beds, and doing our own hair, and remembering to come to tea at the right time?'

'All those things, of course, but I meant something a little different. You see, Harriet, your mother and I wish you to grow up accomplished and ladylike and well-behaved, and your poor mother fears that this won't be possible in a place like this, with no suitable friends, and no governess to look after you. Do you understand?'

'Yes, I think so,' said Harriet, feeling quite wise and elderly.

'Then the way to help your mother is to show her that in spite of these disadvantages, you can still be the kind of person she wants you to be. That means no disobedience, and no bad manners, and certainly no running off on your own. If you turn into a creature as wild as these birds, your mother will insist on our returning home instantly.'

'I promise I won't be unladylike or wild or anything like that,' said Harriet earnestly. 'I only went to Barley Creek yesterday because it was so very important.'

'Of course,' agreed her father. 'And you know, Harriet, I'm rather pleased you did go. I believe I should have gone myself, if you hadn't.'

They smiled at each other, and Harriet could hardly contain her bursting happiness.

'When shall we start school, Father? What time will the classes begin? Did Mr Burnie tell you all about the school?'

'I am to see it for myself, this morning. I understand it's hardly a palace. The classes commence at nine o'clock, and you and Rose-Ann are to come home at half past twelve. Polly will bring you to and from school. As Aidan has already spent a considerable amount of time away from school, it would be best for him to begin attending on Monday, and you and Rose-Ann will go with him. We shall call on Mr and Mrs Farmer on the following Saturday, to arrange for your music lessons. They are in Sydney at present.'

'There's only one thing more I want, Father,' said Harriet, as they followed the path along the fence towards the road and the front garden.

'And what is that? Some breakfast?'

'I *am* hungry, but it's not that. Would we be allowed to play in the back yard sometimes, and watch the cows being milked, and Barrel being fed?'

'I don't see why not, provided you don't annoy Boz or Polly. We shan't be able to afford any more help on the farm or in the house, so they will be our only servants, poor things. We really have enough work here for six or seven.'

He paused at the top of the slope and looked back along the rows of trees.

'We have fifty acres, part of it mere rock and dust. But the property *could* be made to flourish again. Most of these old trees could be dug out. I'm told that this is an excellent district for oranges—I should very much like to try growing them.'

'I could help you,' said Harriet eagerly.

'Perhaps—but remember you will be busy at your lessons. Sometimes, Harriet, I think you should have been the boy in our family.'

And Harriet glowed, recognizing this as one of the finest compliments her father could have paid her.

During breakfast, Mr Wilmot explained the school arrangements to Aidan and Rose-Ann. Aidan was glum and non-committal, while Rose-Ann could not decide whether to be pleased at the prospect of music lessons, or frightened at the thought of school and twenty-one strange children. Mrs Wilmot had the appearance of one who is resigned to her fate, and made no mention of Harriet's visit to Barley Creek. As for Harriet, she ate her porridge and boiled egg and bread and butter with the hearty appetite of an early riser, and minded her manners so scrupulously that even Aidan noticed them.

'Harriet has said "please" six times already,' he observed. 'Has she been out without her sun-bonnet again?'

Harriet glared at him, but nobly suppressed the angry retort which he expected to hear. It was unladylike to quarrel with one's brother.

'I'm pleased to see Harriet is remembering her manners,' said Mrs Wilmot. 'And don't be unkind, Aidan. Now, if we've all finished, I'll ask Polly to clear the table. It's her afternoon off, and there's a great deal of work to be done this morning.'

After tidying her half of the bedroom, Harriet made her way to the cowshed. The two Jerseys had been turned out to graze in the paddock behind the vegetable garden, but Barrel, a sleepy and ageing horse whose name aptly described his shape, was standing in the sun beside the shed, slowly swishing his tail to keep away the flies, and dreaming of the days when he had been Uncle John's smartest carriage horse, and kept always in the glossiest, trimmest condition. Near by, in the part of the shed grandly called the stable, Boz was cleaning the heavy wooden spokes of the buggy, once used by Agnes Wilmot for gentle afternoon drives, and now the sole vehicle on the property.

'Poor old Barrel—never mind,' said Harriet, patting the shaggy neck. 'Some day we'll get a new horse, and you can go and sleep in the paddock all day.'

She wandered into the stable, and leant against the buggy, watching Boz's ever-busy hands. Boz was thin and small, and burnt almost black by the sun. It was impossible to guess his age, but Harriet knew he had been with Uncle John for many years, and that Lillipilly Hill was his only home. He lived in a shack beyond the cow-paddock, and worked from dawn until after dark.

'Good morning, Boz,' said Harriet. 'Did Father tell you we have decided to stay here after all?'

'Told me first thing this mornin',' said Boz, not looking up.

'Aren't you pleased?' asked Harriet curiously.

'Yeah,' said Boz, turning his attention to the harness.

Harriet was not easily discouraged.

'And did Father tell you that we are to go to the Barley Creek school?'

At last Boz glanced up, with a gleam of interest in his dark eyes.

'You and your sister and brother? It's a queer sort of school for you to be goin' to.'

'Why?' demanded Harriet.

But Boz had had enough conversation.

'Time for my cuppa tea,' he muttered, and went out

48

of the shed towards the stone fireplace near the fence. A blackened billy-can hung from a stick above the fire; Boz peered into it, nodded his head, and produced from his trousers pocket a battered tin of tea. Harriet watched respectfully while he threw a handful of tea into the boiling water, then drew off the billy-can with the aid of a forked stick.

'Wouldn't Polly make you some tea in the kitchen?' she asked.

'Wouldn't taste like this,' said Boz contemptuously. He took his tin mug from its hook on the wall of the shed, and filled it with a liquid so black and hot that Harriet shuddered. Then he sat down on the coping of the well, pulled out his ancient pipe, and stared over his mug of tea into the distance.

Harriet realized that Boz's morning break was a hallowed ritual to him, and that he would not welcome any further chatter. So she left him, and strolled away to the side of the cowshed. Here a row of Norfolk Island pines provided welcome shade, and Harriet lingered beneath the graceful tiers of branches, while she surveyed the slope beyond the fence. Somewhere down there was the township, and immediately below must be the church she had seen the day before, but all signs of human life were hidden by the tangle of trees, scrub and vines that covered the hillside.

A sound broke the warm, mid-morning silence, and put to flight a party of blue-wrens and their little brown wives, who had been foraging for insects in a lantana thicket. It was the noise of a branch snapping, and it came from above Harriet's head.

'Don't call out,' said an unknown voice. 'I'm coming down.'

'I wasn't going to call out,' Harriet said. 'Does your mother let you climb trees?'

For the tree-climber was a girl, about Harriet's own age. She slid to the ground with an agility Harriet envied, and dived towards the fence.

'Don't go,' implored Harriet. 'I won't tell anyone you're here.'

The girl paused, eyeing Harriet suspiciously.

'You're the one I saw yesterday, near the school,' Harriet went on eagerly. 'Do you live in Barley Creek?'

'Yes,' said the girl, but she was still wary and unfriendly. She wore the same faded blue frock that Harriet had noticed the day before, and her feet were still bare. Her hair, black and curly, hung around her face in wild disorder, and her skin, like Boz's, was a dark brown. But her eyes were a startling light blue.

'I wish I could climb like you,' said Harriet wistfully.

'Why don't you, then?' demanded the girl rudely.

'We're not allowed. We might tear our clothes.'

'Do you have to wear all those clothes all the time?'

'You mean pinafores and things? I thought everyone had those,' said Harriet, in genuine surprise.

'I don't, then. Silly, I call them,' said the stranger, not without a glance of envy at Harriet's blue hair-ribbon, which Mrs Wilmot had carefully tied after seeing Harriet's own attempts at hairdressing.

Harriet, having been unusually humble until now, thought it was quite time that she asserted herself.

'You don't have to be so rude. That's our tree you were climbing. You might tell me what you were doing.'

'Just climbing,' said the girl defiantly.

Harriet changed her approach. With her customary keen observation, she had noticed the girl's interest in her hair-ribbon.

'If I give you my blue ribbon, will you tell me your name, and what you were doing, and everything?'

'Why do you want to know?' asked the climber, coming a little closer.

'Because I saw you at the school, and I know you live in Barley Creek. You're the first person I've spoken to who goes to that school. You see, we're going there ourselves on Monday.'

'You and your brother and sister?'

'How do you know I've got a brother and sister?' demanded Harriet.

'I know all about you. Polly told Mrs Tolly, and she told Ma. But I didn't know you were going to school. Are you going to give me that ribbon?'

Harriet untied it and smoothed out the creases.

'Tell me first.'

'All right. What do you want to know?'

'Your name, and how old you are, and where you live, and why you were in our tree.'

'Nosy, ain't you?' grumbled the girl. 'I'm Dinny O'Brien, and I'm eleven, and I live up the road from the store—the last house, it is. And I climbed the tree because I wanted to see you and your sister and brother, only I didn't mean for you to see me. Now gimme that ribbon.'

'Dinny isn't a real name,' said Harriet firmly.

'Who says it isn't? That's what I've always been called. It's a better name than yours, anyway. They'll call you Harry at school, just see if they don't.'

'I don't care,' said Harriet. 'And you can have your old ribbon.'

She handed it over, and turned away. She was bitterly disappointed. Here, it seemed, had been a chance, almost literally heaven-sent, to make a friend. Dinny could have been her first friend in this

52

new country, and could have given the Wilmots much valuable help in settling down at the school, and in learning to know the ways of the township.

She had reached the cowshed before she realized that Dinny was following her.

'Wait a minute,' said the girl crossly. 'Don't go so fast. I didn't say we wouldn't be friends. I'll wait for you outside the school on Monday, and if anyone calls you Harry, I'll punch them. But you'd better not be so hoity-toity with the others—they won't like it.'

Boz appeared just then around the corner of the shed, and Dinny vanished in complete silence.

'Boz,' said Harriet, following him into the shed. 'Is there a path down that hill to Barley Creek?'

'Bit of a track,' said Boz. 'Not used much.'

Harriet made an unspoken vow that she would one day find that track, but in the meantime she decided to return to the house and find a fresh hair-ribbon.

At the foot of the back steps she encountered Polly, who had been cleaning out the lean-to bath-house. Polly's round, freckled face was red and damp with heat, but her smile was as broad as ever.

"Mornin', love. I've just heard I've got a new job—takin' you all to school every day. Isn't that brother of yours old enough to look after you?'

'Father says he's so dreamy sometimes he might

53

forget the way,' explained Harriet. 'Polly, do you know a family called O'Brien?'

'In Barley Creek? Oh, everyone knows them. Pinky O'Brien's a splitter—works for Bentley's, over at Winneroo.'

Seeing Harriet's blank expression, Polly set down her bucket and broom, and went on: 'A splitter cuts wood for shingles—you know, like they put on this roof before this new iron was used. There's not so much money in splitting as there used to be, or so they say. Pinky does a bit of sawing as well, and helps with the loads. Bentley's is the biggest mill in these parts—old Bentley has about a hundred men working for him, counting bullockys an' all.'

'Why do the O'Briens live here, then, and not at Winneroo?'

'Because this is where Pinky started working, and built his bit of a house. Not much of a house, either, for all those children.'

'How many?' asked Harriet, fascinated by this picture of Dinny's background.

''Bout six, I think. All boys, but one.'

'And the girl would go to Barley Creek school, wouldn't she?'

'If an O'Brien goes to school, it's only because the law makes him,' declared Polly scornfully. 'They're a wild lot, those O'Briens. And don't you be gettin' too interested in them—your Ma wouldn't like it.'

Remembering how Dinny looked, with her bare brown legs, unkempt hair, and grubby clothes, Harriet was inclined to believe that Polly might be right. However, Harriet found herself thinking quite often of Dinny during that day and the next, and she certainly had no regrets about her lost hair-ribbon.

4

The Bark Schoolhouse

On Sunday night it rained, gently and softly, but when Harriet awoke in the morning, the sunlight was once more struggling through the vines. Peeping through the french window, she could see a low, silver mist wreathed across the garden, with the trees rising above it like the sails of some ghostly ship.

'Get up, Rose-Ann!' she called. 'We're going to school!'

Rose-Ann slowly unwound herself from her bedclothes, and blinked sleepily at her sister.

'Is it cold?'

'Of course not,' said Harriet. 'It's all misty, and still as still. I wish we could go *now*.'

'There wouldn't be anyone else there yet,' said Rose-Ann practically. 'What dresses are we to put on?'

'The green ones, Mother said. I do think it's silly, us always having the same dresses, when we don't look a bit alike. I *hate* my green dress.'

A few minutes later, she surveyed herself as best she could in the cracked looking-glass over the washstand. The green dress had a high neck, trimmed with black braid, and more braid adorned the hem and the too-tight sleeves. The colour seemed to Harriet to make her hair even more sandy, her grey eyes even duller, and her freckles even more prominent. Thankfully she slipped her starched white pinafore over her head, and gave all her attention to the lacing of her boots. The pinafore hid most of the green even if it *was* babyish.

It was most unfair that the identical dress should make Rose-Ann look particularly pretty, and that Aidan, in his Eton suit, should be so neat and scholarly. As they waited at the gate for Polly, after breakfast and last-minute instructions from their parents, Harriet reflected that Mr Burnie should be well pleased with at least two of his pupils.

'Here we are,' said Polly cheerfully, hurrying down the path, shedding her apron as she came. 'My, don't we all look smart!'

Aidan scowled at this compliment. He was still

far from being reconciled to the idea of attending the Barley Creek school, but at least he was prepared to show the other pupils how an English schoolboy should look and behave. He marched off at the head of the procession, with an unnecessary number of books under his arm.

For once Harriet did not glance continually about her, in search of wild flowers and animals and insects. She did lift her head once to listen to the excited chatter of a group of gillbirds, and to watch a formation of black swans pass far above, across the milky sky towards the sea. But for the most part her thoughts raced ahead of her feet, in the direction of the school-house. She wondered whether Dinny would keep her promise, and whether Aidan and Rose-Ann would welcome it.

As they came in sight of the school, Aidan drew even farther away from the rest of the party. To be escorted to school at all was bad enough, but to be conducted thither by a loud-voiced servant-girl was too much of an indignity altogether. He ducked through the sliprail, and stood aloofly under a near-by pine, while Polly took her leave of the girls.

The Wilmots had arrived early, and only half a dozen children were as yet grouped in the shade. Dinny was not one of them. Acutely conscious of six pairs of staring, intensely inquisitive eyes, Harriet yet mustered the courage to gaze at the strange new faces. Five of the children were quite small, ragged, sunburnt little creatures, all barefoot and bareheaded. The sixth was a boy, larger than Aidan, and the proud possessor of a grown-up waistcoat. He was not particularly prepossessing, having a pudgy, sullen face, and bristling hair.

'What's that pile of books for?' he demanded of Aidan, without preamble.

'To read, of course,' said Aidan, his nervousness making him sound more precise and aloof than ever.

The other boy sniggered, and his laughter was echoed dutifully by the younger children. Harriet flushed, and Rose-Ann edged away towards the fence, already entertaining notions of flight.

'We don't wear fancy white collars at this school,' went on the big boy. 'We leave that to the girls —don't we?'

A chorus of assent came from his followers.

'Do you leave your manners behind, too?' asked Aidan, and turned his back on them.

The boy was for a moment baffled, being somewhat slow-witted, and less ready with his tongue than with his fists. One of the smaller children ventured to laugh at Aidan's retort, and that annoyed the big boy still further.

'Don't you speak to me like that!' he bellowed, darting round to peer into Aidan's face. 'What's your name, anyway?'

'Aidan Wilmot. What's yours?'

The other boy ignored the question. He turned delightedly to his followers.

'D'you hear that? Aidan! Will we call him Ada?'

'Ada! Ada!' came the joyful chorus.

Harriet could stand it no longer.

'Hit him, Aidan! Go on—punch him on the nose!'

But Aidan merely shook his head, and strode off towards the schoolhouse.

'He's scared!' said one of the little boys, in a disappointed voice. 'Why don't he fight? He's nearly as big as Paddy.'

'Yeah, your brother's scared,' repeated a small, tow-headed girl at Harriet's elbow.

'He is not!' cried Harriet. 'He just doesn't want to get his hands dirty touching that big bully!'

The boy thus described lifted a hand menacingly, and Rose-Ann began to cry. Harriet, standing her ground, was none the less greatly relieved to see a familiar figure burst through the fence, and to hear Dinny's shout: 'Get away from her, Paddy Tolly, before I go and tell your Ma on you!'

Although Dinny had no supporters, except for two

very small boys clutching her hands, Paddy and his band speedily withdrew, muttering vague threats as they went.

'You don't want to let Paddy scare you,' said Dinny. 'He's as stupid as one of our broody chooks.'

'I wasn't scared,' Harriet declared stoutly.

'But *she* was,' said Dinny, indicating the trembling Rose-Ann. 'And where's your brother?'

'He went inside,' said Harriet, rather shame-facedly. 'He hates people shouting and making scenes.'

'Why didn't he hit Paddy, then? Paddy's all noise—he's not all that good at fighting, though he thinks he is. Here, Pete, stop snivelling!'

The child thus addressed was the smaller of the two—indeed, to Harriet's eyes, he looked as if he should have been at home in the nursery. He was crying quietly to himself, wiping eyes and nose on the grubby sleeve of a jacket several sizes too large for him.

'Pete's only just started school,' Dinny explained. 'He's four. Ma asked Mr Burnie to take him because the baby's sick an' Ma hasn't got much time to look after Pete.'

Rose-Ann was staring at Dinny as if at a creature from another world. Harriet remembered that Dinny was only a year older than Rose-Ann. Compared to the Barley Creek girl, Rose-Ann was hardly more than a baby.

'She's real pretty, your sister, ain't she?' Dinny observed, making Rose-Ann blush. 'How d'you like my ribbon?'

She wore Harriet's ribbon proudly on her tangle of black hair. Her dress was the same washed-out blue as before, but today it was clean.

The hearty clamour of the school bell, hung from a post near the water-tanks, made the Wilmots jump. Since Dinny's arrival, the rest of the pupils had straggled into the grounds, and most of them were grouped at a distance, studying the strangers with frank interest.

'Just stay with me,' ordered Dinny. 'You can sit at my desk.'

Harriet never forgot her first glimpse of the classroom. Over Dinny's shoulder, she could see a floor of rough, uneven planks, bark walls with several chinks through which the sunlight entered, two high windows which failed to give sufficient light, and four rows of battered desks and narrow forms. The only adornments to the room were two coloured religious pictures, a globe, and some large sheets of multiplication tables. Harriet's optimistic spirit quailed a little at the sight of the place to which she had so cheerfully consigned herself and her brother and sister.

Aidan, having not yet been told where to sit, was leaning against the wall beside Mr Burnie's desk. He met the stares of the other pupils with a cool indifference, and refused to respond to Harriet's encouraging smile. That he absolutely loathed his new school, and everyone in it, was only too obvious.

Mr Burnie came in, brisk and smiling, and, to Harriet at least, infinitely reassuring.

'We have three new pupils today,' he told his classes, and the Wilmots immediately became the object of further curious stares. 'Aidan, Harriet, and Rose-Ann Wilmot. They are still strangers in this country, and we should all do our best to make them feel at home. Now, Aidan, as you will be in my top class, you can sit at the end of the back form, next to Bill Mackenzie. The girls seem to have put themselves in the right place, in the middle there. We shall now have our morning reading from the Bible. Your turn, Maggie.'

A plump, red-cheeked girl on Harriet's left stood up, stumbled unhappily through a few verses of Genesis, and sat down hastily and thankfully. While Mr Burnie handed out slates and copy-books, and set his pupils to work, Harriet furtively surveyed her schoolfellows. Of the twenty present, fourteen-year-old Paddy Tolly was the oldest, being kept at school by his widowed mother, the storekeeper, until she decided what to do with him. The youngest was Dinny's brother Pete, now placated with a box-full of assorted buttons, a bodkin, and some wool—equipment which Mr Burnie kept for his smallest pupils, still too young for reading and writing. On the same bench as Pete sat four or five slightly older children, who made up the first and second classes. The next form held half a dozen urchins aged from seven to nine, among them Dinny's other brother, Mick. Harriet's group was made up of seven children—the Wilmots, Dinny, the girl called Maggie, twin boys with bright red hair and identical freckled faces, and another Mackenzie, a shy, frightened creature named Annie. The back form was reserved for what Mr Burnie termed The Rest, boys and girls kept at school for various reasons long after their contemporaries had gone out to work. Aidan and Charles Farmer, still absent, were the only ones interested in higher education. The other four were simply whiling away their time until they could leave school.

Glancing round, Harriet could see Aidan's fair head bent industriously over his books. Next to him, Bill Mackenzie, son of the postmaster, was laboriously spelling out words to himself. His father hoped that Bill would prove capable of passing the Public Service examinations, but Bill lived only for the day when he would be free of school, and perhaps allowed to join the Winneroo fishing fleet. Paddy Tolly stared over the top of his slate at Aidan, no doubt planning his campaign of bullying. Two thirteen-year-old girls on the same bench had been permitted to put aside their slates and do some sewing instead—both were waiting for news of work in two wealthy homes near Blackhill.

'I trust you are not finding our lessons too hard for you, Harriet?' inquired Mr Burnie, pausing beside her desk on one of his endless rounds. 'You don't appear to have done very much writing.'

Harriet turned red, and bent over her copy-book. Rose-Ann had been writing in her best copperplate for some minutes, and even Dinny had achieved an erratic row of letters. Mr Burnie's hold over his remarkably assorted bunch of pupils was very firm, and the most reluctant scholars could not fail to leave his school without learning at least the elements of reading, writing, and adding up.

When the mid-morning break came, Harriet did not know whether to be pleased or anxious. Here in the schoolroom all was peaceful and orderly, under Mr Burnie's vigilant eye. In the playground, Paddy Tolly and his band could no doubt find ways of evading the schoolmaster, and do more or less as they pleased.

'Where are we going?' Harriet asked, as Dinny steered the two Wilmot girls across the playground.

'You'll see,' said Dinny mysteriously. There seemed few private spots indeed in that bare stretch of ground, but Dinny, with her usual resourcefulness, had found one. Right against the boundary fence, beneath a clump of turpentines, stood an old, disused tank, lying on its side. The top had rusted away, leaving an opening facing the bush, and hidden from the playground.

'Go on—get in,' urged Dinny.

Harriet needed no further persuasion, but Rose-Ann hung back, peering doubtfully at the square iron cavern, thickly carpeted with fallen leaves.

'Are there any spiders?' she asked.

'Only little ones,' Dinny assured her. 'They don't bite.'

Rose-Ann crept unhappily into the tank, and sat down as close to the entrance as she could.

'This is my own place,' Dinny said proudly. 'Maggie and Annie can come here, but no one else. So swear you won't tell the others about it.'

Harriet and Rose-Ann promised readily. Harriet had begun to realize that Dinny was quite a personage in the Barley Creek school, and that the bestowal of her friendship was something of an honour. Rose-Ann, understanding none of this, stared in wonderment at Dinny's bare feet.

'Don't your feet get cold?' she asked innocently.

''Course not,' said Dinny contemptuously. 'It's warm, ain't it? When it's cold I'll wear Joe's old boots.'

'Who's Joe?' demanded Harriet.

'My brother—the second biggest one. He helps Pa with the cutting, and he has to have boots, 'cause of the snakes. Last one they killed was six foot long, Joe says.'

'Do they eat people, those snakes?' asked Rose-Ann, in horrified fascination.

'No—but they bite people. One of Pa's mates got bit once, on the leg, and Pa had to cut the leg open with his knife, to let the poison out. The man was awful sick for a while.'

Harriet shivered. How difficult it was to believe that only a few short months ago she had been leading a sedate and quiet life in Kensington, where snakes were merely creatures shown in picture-books! And what would her acquaintances there have made of Dinny O'Brien? It would have taken much more than a fear of snakes, however, to have sent Harriet back to her former existence, so dull by comparison with the present.

Rose-Ann was feeling quite the opposite.

'I wish we could go home,' she wailed.

Dinny at once became protective, as she was always to be with Rose-Ann. Harriet she treated as an equal.

'Don't you fret about those snakes. They wouldn't ever bite *you*.'

'It's not just the snakes,' said Rose-Ann dismally. 'It's being so lonely, and having to go to this queer school, and there's that awful boy who called Aidan names—'

'I didn't like school much at first,' said Dinny. 'I didn't go till I was eight, and that was when Ma found out it was the law, that we all had to go to school. But now I think it's better than being at home, looking after the babies, and helping pick beans and peas, and doing the washing. And that Paddy Tolly won't call your brother names if your brother turns round and hits him in the eye.'

'Aidan's no good at fighting,' said Harriet.

'He'd better learn, then. Joe'll teach him, next time he's home. And Tim—that's the biggest one, him that's working for the butcher in Blackhill—Tim once hit a boy so hard he was asleep for a week.'

Harriet was to learn that Dinny's tales were not always strictly accurate, but she always enjoyed them. She was about to demand more O'Brien family history when the bell sounded.

'Come on,' said Dinny. 'It's a long run from here, and Mr Burnie hates us to be late.'

As Harriet hurried breathlessly into the schoolroom, she noticed that Aidan was sitting quietly in his place, and that neither he nor Paddy Tolly showed signs of wear and tear. She didn't know whether to be pleased or sorry.

The next half-hour was devoted to a singing lesson, which cheered Rose-Ann somewhat, especially as the song was one she already knew, and Mr Burnie invited her to sing it alone to the class. Rose-Ann, had she but realized it, was well on the way to becoming popular with her classmates. Her prettiness and her good clothes roused little envy in the hearts of the other girls, who for the most part were content to remain as they were, and her anxious desire to please was quite obvious. Harriet, having been adopted by Dinny, was more or less accepted. But Aidan puzzled everybody. Tough and independent as they were, the Barley Creek children looked askance at a boy who did not seem to show the same qualities. So they withdrew from Aidan in a body, and waited to see what he would do.

All this Harriet dimly guessed at, and despite her own successful morning, she was troubled as she joined Polly and the others at the sliprail at the beginning of the dinner-hour. Aidan was to have his midday meal at home, and although he tried to avoid his sisters during the walk, Harriet eventually caught up with him under the lillipillies at the gate.

'Where did you go at break this morning?' she asked.

'Nowhere,' said Aidan. 'I stayed inside and talked to Mr Burnie.'

'Do you like him?'

'He's a good teacher,' admitted Aidan. 'But really, Harriet, why you ever thought we ought to go to this school is beyond me. I wouldn't stay another minute if Father hadn't said I must at least try it.'

'Why?' asked Harriet, daringly.

'Why? Can't you *see*? It's more like a—a—prison than a school, with those awful bare walls, and no equipment, and the pupils look like convicts, too. And imagine having to go to school with *girls*!'

Heroically, Harriet decided to ignore this last remark.

'But you won't be there so long, you know—not if you win that scholarship.'

'I'll win it all right—if I can stay till then,' said Aidan bitterly, and he marched off towards the house, kicking at the pebbles as he went.

Harriet followed slowly, gazing ahead at the spreading iron roof and the golden stone walls of her new home. She now loved every part of it, even the cheerless bedroom, which she was planning to decorate to her own taste. She loved the guardian lillipillies, and the shaggy garden, and the pungently-scented gums, and above all she loved the broad, clear view of blue hills and shadowy gullies. How could Aidan be so indifferent to all these things?

During the meal, Aidan answered his parents' questions about school with single syllables, and pretended not to see the deepening frown on his father's face. But Harriet was only too well aware of it.

'We think the school is excellent, don't we, Rose-Ann?' she said primly, at the same time kicking her sister on the ankle.

'Yes,' agreed Rose-Ann dutifully, though she was hardly able to conceal her delight at the thought of a quiet afternoon alone with her mother.

Harriet sighed. It was unfair, she reflected, that so much should depend on Aidan, who even now looked quite ill at the prospect of returning to school in half an hour's time, while she herself could hardly wait until the next morning.

'What are we to do after our rest, Mother?' she asked.

'I think perhaps you had better finish your embroidery,' said Mrs Wilmot firmly. 'You should have something to show Mrs Burnie when you begin your lessons with her.'

It was the answer that Harriet had expected, after all. And if everything went well, she would still have an hour's daylight in which to read *Treasure Island*, and to forget the problem of Aidan for a time.

5

More about Barley Creek

For the remainder of that week, Aidan managed to avoid Paddy Tolly, at least during school hours. And Paddy was sufficiently in awe of Polly to refrain from taunting his victim while she was present. So Aidan went unmolested—and friendless. The other boys, disappointed because he would not face up to Paddy, and puzzled by his distant manner, simply left him alone. He spoke to no one at school save Mr Burnie, and concentrated fiercely on his lessons, at which he did so well that Mr Burnie was obliged to send for more books for him. Unfortunately, this failed to impress his schoolfellows.

Meanwhile, Harriet was beginning to feel that she had been attending the Barley Creek school all her life, so familiar and friendly had it become. And even Rose-Ann admitted that it was not as bad as she had expected.

On the Friday morning Harriet had a further glimpse into the family life of the O'Briens. During the break, Pete fell and cut his knee, and, after tying on a bandage, Mr Burnie told Dinny to take him home, and leave him there for the rest of the day.

'Can Harriet come with us?' asked Dinny.

Mr Burnie hesitated. Though to all outward appearances he treated the Wilmots exactly as he treated his other pupils, he watched over them with just a little more care. He liked Francis Wilmot, and he understood the other man's desire that his children should not suffer from their changed way of life. He realized, too, how important it was to Mrs Wilmot that her daughters should not be turned into hoydens. He had had a few misgivings about Harriet's friendship with Dinny.

'Very well,' he said at last. 'But be back in fifteen minutes, mind.'

Delighted with their sudden freedom, Harriet and Dinny hurried along the road, towing Pete between them. It was the first time that Harriet had been beyond the post office, and she looked around her with keen interest. There was not a great deal to see. The hard white road stretched gradually uphill, overhung by grey-green wattles and bordered by the stiff, sharp clumps that Dinny called 'sword-grass'. Occasionally a break in the trees revealed a sliprail, and the twin ruts of a cart-track, but no houses were visible from the road.

'This is the way to Deacon's Flat,' said Dinny. 'It's about six mile out. Our place is just round the corner.'

A curve in the road brought them to a rough clearing on the edge of a forest of bluegums. The clearing had been crudely fenced with forked posts and sagging wire, across which the indomitable blackberries thrust their prickly tendrils.

'Time Pa came home and chopped those blackberries out,' observed Dinny, helping Pete through the fence. 'Ma and me can't do a thing with 'em. Don't walk on our bean plants.'

The patch of ground in front of the house had been made into a vegetable garden. There were no flowers, but a thick mat of Wandering Jew stretched on either side of the sawn-off stump that did duty as a doorstep.

'Come on in,' invited Dinny, as Pete limped ahead of them, calling for his mother. 'Ma won't mind.'

The house was of unpainted timber, with a shingle roof patched here and there with iron. Harriet followed Dinny through the open door into what appeared to

75

be the family living-room. As Harriet was to discover, the house boasted only three rooms, and this one served as dining-room, kitchen, bathroom, and parlour. A huge chimney covered most of one wall, with a rusty stove beneath it. Sacks lay here and there on the uneven wood floor, and more sacking hung over one of the two small windows. The other window was the only one in the house which had a complete pane of glass.

In front of the stove, Dinny's mother was bathing the baby in a battered tin tub. She was a small woman, not much bigger than Dinny, and stooped from continual hard work. She stared in astonishment at her daughter and the visitor—as Harriet later found out, visitors were extremely rare in the O'Brien household.

'What's the matter, Dinny? Are you sick?'

'No, it's Pete—he cut hisself,' explained Dinny, looking round for her brother, who, having reassured himself of his mother's presence, had retired into a corner with a handful of blackberries picked on the way home.

'And are you going back to school? Who's this?' Mrs O'Brien asked, indicating Harriet.

'That's Harriet Wilmot—you know, from up the hill. I told you about her. Can we have something to eat?'

'There's bread an' dripping on the table,' said Mrs O'Brien, still looking at Harriet, studying her white pinafore and polished boots with embarrassing interest.

Dinny brought Harriet a thick slice of freshly baked bread, lavishly spread with mutton fat, and sprinkled with salt and pepper. Harriet, feeling distinctly awkward and unwelcome, gazed uncertainly at this delicacy.

'Eat it,' commanded Dinny, between mouthfuls. 'There's lots more for our dinner.'

Harriet did as she was bid, and found the snack quite the tastiest she had ever had.

'I'll ask Polly to give me some when I go home,' she said. 'It's her baking day.'

'You'll have something better than that for your dinner, I'll be bound,' declared Mrs O'Brien matter-of-factly. 'But I'm sure Polly Hopkins's dripping's no nicer than ours, all the same.'

'What's the baby's name?' asked Harriet, peering at the child with polite interest. Unlike Rose-Ann, who still cherished a whole family of dolls, Harriet was not fond of babies, and this one seemed a rather meagre and unattractive specimen.

'That's our Steve,' said Mrs O'Brien proudly, lifting the child from the tub and setting him on a sack to dry him. 'It's hard work thinking of names for all these boys, I can tell you. Naming Dinny was a real treat. Diana Elizabeth Agnes, she is—it was the prettiest name I could think of. It's a pity she ain't pretty to go with it.'

Dinny was quite unconcerned by this remark, but Harriet came loyally to her friend's defence.

'Oh, but she is pretty! See how curly her hair is!'

'Well, she'll have to do, I suppose,' said Dinny's mother. 'I hear you Wilmots are here to stay—is that right?'

'Yes,' answered Harriet, surprised by the directness of the question. Apparently the entire township knew of the Wilmots' affairs.

'It's a bit lonely for your mother, I reckon. The other Mrs Wilmot used to drive round in her buggy, visiting all her friends. An' she'd spend weeks in Sydney, sometimes. But then she had no children to think of.'

Mrs O'Brien seemed ready to talk all morning, and it was with some difficulty that Harriet managed to edge away.

'We'll be late if we don't go now,' she said. 'Thank you very much for the bread.'

'No trouble,' Mrs O'Brien assured her, following them to the door, with Steve tucked under one arm. 'Come again.'

'Ma likes to talk,' said Dinny, as they hurried back along the road. 'Last person to visit was a swaggie, an' he never said a word. Ma must of took to you straight off—telling you my real name an' everything.'

'I like your mother,' said Harriet thoughtfully, as they crossed the playground. There was no more time to talk, as the bell rang just then, but Harriet did not soon forget her meeting with Mrs O'Brien. Somehow the bareness and poorness of the house in the clearing ceased to matter, when she remembered Mrs O'Brien's cheerful good spirits.

On the following day, which was Saturday, Harriet paid a visit of a very different nature. This was to the Rectory, a full-dress occasion demanding white muslins and coloured sashes and cotton gloves, all of which Harriet hated, and Rose-Ann relished. As the buggy would only hold three in any comfort, Mr and Mrs Wilmot and Rose-Ann drove, while Aidan and Harriet walked.

It was a still, grey, clouded afternoon, humid and heavy with the promise of rain. The bush was completely quiet.

'I'd much rather walk, anyway,' said Harriet with satisfaction. 'It will make our visit shorter, too. Did Father tell you, Aidan, that Polly isn't to take us to school any more? He says we are old enough to look after ourselves, and Polly's too busy.'

Aidan frowned. Much as he disliked being escorted by a servant-girl, he had to admit that Polly's presence gave him a certain amount of protection from his tormentors, from Paddy Tolly in particular. Harriet was quite shrewd enough to read his thoughts.

'But from Monday Charles Farmer will be back at school, and you could go some of the way with him. I know a much shorter path to school, and it goes past the church.'

'How did you find it?' asked Aidan, with some interest.

'Dinny showed me. It goes down the hill near the cowshed. Only it's all overgrown.'

'We could ask Boz to clear it,' suggested Aidan.

'We could clear it ourselves,' said Harriet sturdily. 'It would be worth the trouble, wouldn't it?'

And Aidan had to agree that it would.

Barley Creek seemed to be totally deserted. School, store, and post office were all blank-faced and silent, and no horses were tied beneath the peppercorn tree on the little patch of grass below the church—that patch being the meeting-place of the township. In the hushed grey and green landscape, the only brightness was in the Rectory poplars, already turning gold.

'I wonder what Charles is like,' said Harriet, as they opened the Rectory gate. Aidan, who had been thinking exactly the same thing, said nothing—more discreet than Harriet, he realized that they were within earshot of the wide-open windows. The Rectory was a grey timber house, with steep gables decorated with what looked like white wooden frills.

Harriet intensely disliked the kind of visit where she had to sit very still and straight in a high-backed chair, and speak only when she was addressed directly. Worse still was the afternoon tea-party at which she might be suddenly called upon to recite, or sing, or play the piano. So she was greatly relieved to find that the Farmers were kind, informal people, and that the children were allowed to stay out of doors while the grown-ups talked in the sitting-room.

'Let's go in the summer-house,' said Charles, leading the way up the sloping back garden to the little wooden shelter at the top. From here one could gaze down past the house to the township, and beyond to the creek and the encircling hills.

'Watch for spiders,' said Charles solemnly to Rose-Ann. 'I think you might be sitting on one.'

Rose-Ann at once jumped up in great alarm, and Charles burst into hearty laughter. He was a plump, good-natured, cheerful boy, a born tease, and always ready to bubble over with amusement.

'Rose-Ann doesn't think spiders are funny,' Aidan explained. 'She hasn't been here long enough for that. Sit down, Rose-Ann—it was only a joke.'

'Haven't you any sisters I could play with?' asked Rose-Ann hopefully.

'No sisters, or brothers either,' said Charles. 'And I must say I'm pleased you've come here to live. It's been so dull at school lately, with only Paddy and Bill to talk to. They're hopeless at cricket, too. Do you bowl or bat?' he demanded eagerly of Aidan.

'I've not played much,' admitted Aidan.

'You'll soon learn,' Charles assured him. 'If you're good enough, you might be allowed to join the Barley Creek side next summer. The season's nearly over now. Our last match is with Deacon's Flat, on Saturday.'

'Do you mean *you* play for Barley Creek?' asked Harriet in surprise. Her knowledge of cricket was even less than Aidan's, and she envisaged an eleven as being made up of tall, serious gentlemen with beards.

'Of course I do,' said Charles airily. 'I'm one of the opening bats, usually. Joe O'Brien's the other, when he's home. Why don't you come and watch next Saturday?'

'We shall, if Father will take us,' said Harriet with enthusiasm.

Charles turned again to Aidan.

'How do you like the school? I've been there four years, and I'm used to it. But I suppose it must look rather odd to you, after being at school in London.'

'It's all right,' said Aidan. 'I wish I could go to the Grammar School sooner, though.'

'Whatever for?' demanded Charles. 'You'll have to work much harder there. And you won't be able to go fishing or exploring or hunting rabbits after school. I shot four rabbits yesterday.'

'Aidan doesn't do any of those things, anyway,' explained Harriet, adding wistfully: 'But I would like to.'

'Girls make too much noise when you're after rabbits or fish,' said Charles. 'I could take you exploring, though. I know where a platypus lives, and there's a whole family of bush cats up in the hill behind O'Brien's place.'

'Harriet wouldn't be allowed,' said Rose-Ann.

'What's a platypus?' asked Harriet.

'It has feet like a duck, and fur, and it swims in the creek. And I know where the bunyip lives, too. A bunyip,' he went on, addressing the wide-eyed Rose-Ann, 'is huge and black, and it howls like this—'

He threw back his head and emitted a cry so blood-curdling that Rose-Ann turned quite pale.

'There are no such things as bunyips,' said Harriet triumphantly. 'Polly says so.'

'No one's ever *seen* one,' admitted Charles. 'All the same, Bill Mackenzie's absolutely sure that one lives in the cave on Maloney's Hill—he's heard it.'

'Bill Mackenzie would say anything,' said Aidan scornfully.

'Don't you like him, then?' asked Charles curiously. 'He's awfully slow, but he wouldn't hurt a fly.'

'I don't like any of them,' muttered Aidan.

Puzzled, Charles stood up.

'Come on, I'll show you my pet bandicoot. His name's Sniffy.'

Sniffy proved to be a rather disappointing creature, being sound asleep in a dark corner underneath the house, and most unwilling to be disturbed. All that was visible was a mound of greyish fur and the tip of a long snout. But Rose-Ann was content to linger and gaze at him, and even plucked up courage to pat his unresponsive back.

Aidan disappeared into the house, and Charles and Harriet were left alone in the quiet garden.

'What's your brother so bad-tempered about?' inquired Charles. 'He doesn't seem to like anything.'

Harriet explained about Paddy Tolly and his friends, adding in conclusion: 'So you see, all the others are waiting to see what Aidan will do. Only I think he'll just do nothing. He hates fighting.'

'I'd punch Paddy myself, if it would help,' said Charles cheerfully. 'But that wouldn't make any difference. Aidan will have to do it. He's nearly as big as Paddy, and Paddy's a coward, anyway. There wouldn't be much fighting, really.'

Harriet stared thoughtfully at the lace gables and at a row of magpies spaced at exactly equal intervals along the ridge-pole.

'Something will have to be done soon,' she declared. 'If Aidan tells Father that he absolutely hates this school, then Father might decide we ought to go back to London after all. We're to give it a six months' trial, you see, and it matters much more about Aidan than about Rose-Ann and me.'

Charles sincerely wanted to help. He liked Harriet, and although he privately considered Aidan more than a little foolish, he still hoped that the other boy might prove to be a good companion. Charles loved company, and friends of his own age were scarce in Barley Creek.

'I think you ought to stay,' he said. 'I can't see why anyone would want to go back to London after this. I don't remember much about it myself, but I'm sure it was awfully dull. If I arranged things so that Aidan just *had* to fight Paddy, would that help? I'm certain he'd beat Paddy easily, and then all the others would think a lot of Aidan, and he'd soon get to like the school.'

'It sounds quite a good idea,' said Harriet gratefully. 'Do you think you can do it?'

'Just leave it to me,' said Charles confidently, and Harriet went in to tea feeling that she had found a staunch ally.

Next morning, as she dressed for church, Harriet began to have a few misgivings.

'Rose-Ann,' she said to her sister, who was lacing her boots with an air of intense concentration, 'has Aidan ever fought anyone before?'

'Before when?' asked Rose-Ann in surprise.

'Oh, no time in particular,' said Harriet hastily. 'I was only wondering.'

'I've never heard him talk about any fights he had,' said Rose-Ann. 'You know how he loathes scenes, and ugly things. If you're ready, could you do my boots for me? I can't make them go right.'

Had Harriet walked alone again with Aidan that morning, her conscience would probably have forced her into telling him all about Charles's plan, thereby giving him a chance to avoid the coming fight, or at least prepare himself for it. But today Mr Wilmot decided to walk, leaving Boz to drive, with the two girls squeezed into a space meant for one.

'Couldn't I walk home, Mother?' pleaded Harriet. 'It's so hot like this.'

'I haven't heard you complain of the heat before, Harriet,' said her mother. 'It's much more suitable for young ladies to ride than to walk. I only wish we could have a real carriage, with room enough for all of us.'

Poor Mrs Wilmot was trying very hard to like her new surroundings, knowing that her husband wished to make Lillipilly Hill their permanent home. But she could not help but find it strange to be driving to church in a somewhat ancient open buggy, with a hard leather seat, under a blazing sun whose heat seemed to grow no less fierce although it was already autumn. Autumn, however, meant little here where the trees were almost all ever-greens, and in any case, how could one associate early April with any season but spring?

Word had been passed around that the Wilmots were to make their first appearance at the church that morning, and the tiny stone building was quite full as the family walked in single file to their pew at the front. Heads turned openly as they passed, and many a feminine gaze was directed at Mrs Wilmot's bright blue taffeta gown, with its fashionable tulle overskirt, and her small beribboned hat. Harriet glimpsed a few familiar faces—Bill and Annie Mackenzie sat with their parents, and Paddy Tolly, in his best suit, accompanied his mother, a fat, comfortable-looking woman who knew the entire family history of everyone in the district.

Charles and his mother were just across the aisle from the Wilmots, and the grin that Charles gave to Harriet was that of a fellow-conspirator. Harriet tried to concentrate on the service, but occasionally she would glance sideways at Aidan, so handsome and tidy in his Sunday clothes, and think of the burly Paddy only a few yards away. It hardly seemed a fair match.

'I'll speak to Charles afterwards,' Harriet decided, fumbling through the hymn-book to find the place, 'and tell him I've changed my mind about the fight.'

As they left the church, however, they were met by a small reception committee of Barley Creek folk, led by Mrs Tolly.

'We've been wanting to say how-d'ye-do,' said the storekeeper, beaming. 'We've not had a chance so far. But we've heard all about you from the children at school. Paddy here sits on the same bench as your boy, don't you, Paddy?'

Paddy muttered something unintelligible, and

escaped to the farthest corner of the churchyard. Harriet looked round for Charles, only to see him climbing through the fence that divided the church from the Rectory. Mrs Tolly's voice flowed evenly on, while Mrs Wilmot made polite rejoinders, and Mr Mackenzie took it upon himself to explain to Mr Wilmot just what Lillipilly Hill needed in the way of agricultural development. The children shifted from foot to foot, longing to be off, until a remark of Mr Mackenzie's finally caught their attention.

'And another thing,' said the postmaster. 'There's a rumour of a bushranger being in the district. I don't believe it myself—hasn't been a bushranger here for about ten years. There's not enough in it for them now that most of the big mills have shut down, and the roads have opened up the district. But better keep your doors locked, and your stock penned in.'

'Our stock consists of two cows and one horse,' said Mr Wilmot with a rueful smile. 'Still, I'll take your advice—we can't afford to lose them.'

'And do please call on us whenever you wish,' added his wife, moving gradually towards the waiting buggy. 'We are seldom away from home. Come along, children.'

Harriet had forgotten Aidan and Paddy for the time being. In the buggy she turned eagerly to Boz.

'Boz, do you think it's true about the bushranger? Mr Mackenzie said he'd heard of one. What do bush-rangers *do*?'

'Gee-up, there!' Boz called to Barrel, who did not alter his leisurely pace in the least. 'I reckon there ain't any bushranger within fifty mile of here. Wilsons out on Deacon's Flat Road lost a few chickens, and someone else lost some apples off their trees, but that could've been swaggies.'

'Do bushrangers ride big black horses, and rob rich people to help the poor?' asked Harriet hopefully.

Boz uttered a sort of grunt which was his only form of laughter.

'Not on your life! Just common thieves, they are, and born to be hung, most of 'em. Cut your throat for two-pence, more than likely.'

'Really, Harriet, this hardly seems a subject for you to be discussing,' said Mrs Wilmot. 'You're fright-ening Rose-Ann.'

'Everything frightens *her*,' muttered Harriet rebel-liously, deciding to question Boz further when he was alone in the cowshed. The rest of the drive was made in silence, broken only by Boz's whistling of some tune which might or might not have been *The Wild Colonial Boy.*

After the midday meal, a lengthy affair involving a leg of lamb—the only fresh meat served during the week—and some of Polly's stickiest treacle tart, Harriet felt too sleepy to do anything more energetic than retire to the side veranda with *Treasure Island*. It was tea-time before she thought again of Aidan and the fight, and by that time her conscience had been dulled. On Sundays Aidan stayed up to have supper with his parents, so Harriet went to bed without having mentioned Charles's plan to anyone.

'After all,' she told herself drowsily, as she lay in bed listening to the mournful night-song of a mopoke, 'I can always tell him in the morning. That will be time enough.'

6

The Scheme that Failed

Aidan was not in an approachable mood next morning. The quiet Saturday and Sunday, with their generous opportunities for the reading and idling which he so much enjoyed, had been greatly to his taste. By contrast, Monday had nothing to offer but further dreary, lonely hours of school, and the contempt of his schoolfellows. Too proud by far to show his sisters how miserable he was, he stalked ahead of them down the hill, his books clutched tightly to his chest.

'It's a lovely morning,' said Harriet tentatively, skipping down beside him.

Indeed it was. The sky had suddenly lost its harshness, and the wind from the south breathed a seasonable coolness. It ruffled the plumes of the tree-ferns, and set the shadowed creek dancing over the pebbles of the ford. A Jacky Winter hopped and sang cheerfully beside the path; Rose-Ann searched her pinafore pocket for crumbs, and lingered to watch him gather them.

'I suppose it is,' said Aidan indifferently. 'All the mornings seem the same here.'

'Oh, but they're not—' began Harriet, then stopped. This was not the time to be argumentative. She went on, in sudden inspiration: 'Don't you feel well? Shall I go back and tell Mother you ought to stay at home?'

'Of course not,' said Aidan crossly. 'Do stop fussing, Harriet. I'm quite all right. You don't usually worry about my health.'

'But I *am* worried,' insisted Harriet. 'I just have a queer feeling that you shouldn't go to school today.'

Aidan stopped and turned to look at her.

'Why?' he demanded suspiciously.

Harriet refused to meet the accusing stare of her brother's clear, blue eyes.

'I don't know,' she mumbled. 'You might get into trouble, or get hurt, or something.'

'You're being ridiculous,' said Aidan scornfully. 'It will be just another dull old day, with no one decent to talk to.'

'There's Charles, don't forget,' said Harriet. 'You like Charles, don't you?'

'Yes,' answered Aidan, without enthusiasm. Charles, he felt, was more likely to be friendly with Bill or Paddy than with him—the Barley Creek boys had much more in common with the minister's son than did the studious youth newly arrived from England.

'Charles likes *you*,' said Harriet, feeling a little desperate now, for the schoolhouse was already in sight. 'He wants to help you.'

'I don't want anyone's help, thank you,' said Aidan coldly, and walked rapidly away.

Harriet sighed. She knew she could have been more tactful, but discretion was not her strong point. And Aidan had been even more prickly than she had expected. All she could do now was stand back and wait.

She did not have to wait long. At break Charles came up to her with a look of triumph on his round, brown face.

'It's all arranged. It was a bit difficult, but I managed it. The fight's on after school this afternoon, in the clearing at the back of Tolly's. Bill's to be in charge.'

'Whatever did you say to Aidan?' asked Harriet, glancing round for her brother, who was nowhere in sight.

'I just told him Paddy wanted to fight him—that's true enough, isn't it?—and where Paddy would be at four o'clock. He'll have to come.'

'I wish we hadn't done it,' said Harriet miserably. 'It seems so mean, now.'

'Of course it's not,' declared Charles. 'It's the best thing that could happen. Aidan won't get hurt at all—you'll see.'

But how was she to see? This was the problem which beset Harriet all morning, so seriously that her lessons were neglected, and Mr Burnie stood her out in front of the class for ten minutes, as a penalty for being inattentive.

As soon as the morning classes were over, Harriet consulted Rose-Ann. Harriet knew that their first music lesson with Mrs Farmer had been arranged for that afternoon, but she had not been sufficiently interested to find out all the details.

'What time do we have to be at the Rectory, Rose-Ann?'

'Half past two,' said her sister. 'Mrs Farmer will give us each half an hour, then Polly will come and take us home.'

Trailing along the dusty road, watching Aidan striding silently ahead, Harriet set her ready mind to work.

'Let's see, then—if we made each lesson last longer than half an hour, and kept Polly waiting a little, we could leave the Rectory just before four o'clock. I wonder how long the fight will take?'

'What *are* you talking about?' demanded Rose-Ann.

'Aidan's fighting Paddy Tolly after school today,' Harriet explained. 'And we *must* see it.'

Rose-Ann gaped at her.

'Why must we? I don't want to, not a bit. However did poor Aidan get into a fight?'

'Never mind that,' said Harriet impatiently. 'We have to be there, to cheer Aidan on. We're his sisters, aren't we? Now listen, Rose-Ann—you must play all the pieces you know for Mrs Farmer, and I'll make lots of mistakes. That should make the lessons last longer. Then we'll watch the fight, and go home by the back way, up the hill. Dinny showed it to me, and it's much quicker.'

As always, Rose-Ann became a reluctant partner to Harriet in her well-laid scheme. To Mrs Farmer's mild surprise, Rose-Ann went through her entire repertoire of piano pieces, including several which she had not yet completely mastered.

'I thought she was such a quiet, retiring little thing,' Mrs Farmer remarked afterwards to her husband. 'But she almost insisted on playing everything she knew—she even gave me some pieces twice. Fortunately she plays quite nicely—not like poor Harriet. That child will never be musical.'

It was not at all difficult for Harriet to make mistakes that afternoon. She was not at the best of times an accomplished performer, and today, with the thought of Aidan's ordeal continually on her mind, she alternately rushed and stumbled through her pieces in a manner that made Mrs Farmer shudder. While Rose-Ann sat at the piano, rendering a Haydn minuet, with her fair, curly head bent over the keyboard, and the tip of her tongue protruding as a sign of intense concentration, Harriet perched on the edge of an uncomfortable, straight-backed chair, staring at what was visible of the outside world between the heavy green plush curtains of the sitting-room window. How was Aidan feeling now? Was Paddy leering at him over his book? Would Bill Mackenzie see that all was fair and properly conducted?

'Excuse me, Mrs Farmer,' she said politely, suddenly noticing a familiar figure on the front path, 'would you mind if I went out and told Polly we might be a little late?'

'Certainly you may go and speak to Polly,' said Mrs Farmer. 'But there is no need for you to be late. You have had your full time.'

'Couldn't we play our duet for you?' asked Harriet. 'Polly won't mind waiting.'

Rose-Ann plunged dutifully into a Mozart waltz as Harriet hurried outside. It did not take her long to explain the situation to Polly, nor was Polly slow to offer her help.

'You mean our Aidan's fighting that fat Tolly boy? I always hoped he would. Of course we must all go and cheer for him—don't you worry. You go back to your pianner, and I'll go and talk to Sarah.'

Sarah, the Rectory maid, was a girl of Polly's own age, and she could be depended upon to provide a cup of tea and plenty of gossip for her friend. It was ten minutes to four when Mrs Farmer finally rose from her chair beside the piano.

'You girls really must go home now. It's growing quite late. And don't forget to practise your scales and exercises—you especially, Harriet.'

The township was very quiet as Polly and her charges made their way back to the school. Mrs Tolly was sitting in the slanting sunlight at the front door of the store, which was empty of customers.

'What's happened to all the schoolchildren?' she demanded of Polly. 'Store's always full of 'em at this time of day.'

'Must of found something else to do,' said Polly cheerfully. 'Come on, girls.'

They followed the road well past the schoolhouse, then turned aside into the scrub. The noisy chatter of a dozen young voices guided them to a leaf-strewn clearing among the gums and wattles. Most of Mr Burnie's pupils had come to see the fray, and had perched themselves in a rough circle on stumps and fallen branches. Dinny was there, with a small brother on either side, and Charles leant against a blackbutt, talking earnestly with Bill.

The appearance of the Lillipilly Hill party caused a sudden lull in the general conversation.

'I didn't think you'd be let come,' said Dinny. 'Come over here by me.'

Harriet crossed the ring to join Dinny on her log, but Rose-Ann, pink with embarrassment at all the curious stares, chose to stay with Polly, who, as the only near-adult present, was being surveyed with some suspicion.

'Don't fret about me,' said Polly. 'I'm here to watch, same as you. Where are they?'

Knowing quite well to whom she referred, Charles answered: 'Paddy's here, behind Bill. Aidan hasn't come yet.'

'D'you reckon he *will* come?' asked Dinny of Harriet.

'Of course he will,' said Harriet stoutly, although she was not at all sure that she really wanted Aidan to appear. The circle of expectant faces, the tense feeling in the air, the hefty, solid shape of Paddy, now emerging into the centre of the ring, all combined to make her wish with all her sinking heart that she had never asked Charles to arrange the affair. But when at last Aidan came along the path between the tall trees, looking—whatever he felt—calm and unruffled, she felt a glow of pride. A few of the onlookers clapped. Now that Aidan had shown himself willing to meet Paddy in fair fight, as they thought, most of the children were ready to take his side. A new leader, after Paddy's long rule, would not have been unwelcome.

Aidan glanced briefly at his sisters, nodded to Bill, and took off his jacket. Polly stepped forward to hold it.

'You show 'im what you can do,' she whispered encouragingly. 'We'll cheer for you.'

Aidan smiled at her. He was very pale, and, as Polly declared afterwards, ''e was shaking like a jelly, all over.'

There were no preliminaries. Bill simply motioned Aidan forward into the centre, and stood aside. Paddy, frowning most ferociously, charged at Aidan like a bull at a gate. Aidan side-stepped, and even managed to land a light blow on Paddy's ear as Paddy rushed past. But as Aidan turned again, he tripped, and landed on his knees. At once Paddy was upon him, using his hammer-like fists, regardless of the angry yells of the onlookers.

Shielding himself as best he could, Aidan scrambled to his feet. He rubbed his hand over his face, and stood for a moment staring at the blood smearing his palm. Then he looked at Paddy. The other boy was ready to charge again, seeing that his opponent was temporarily dazed. Aidan put his head down and ran from the ring, past the startled Harriet, and disappeared into the darkening bush.

After a moment of astonished silence, everyone began to talk at once.

'He's scared stiff! He's run away!'

'What a fight! Anyone else want to try?'

'Gee, one of the girls 'ud have done better!'

But Dinny stood up on top of her log, and made her voice heard above the clamour.

'It wasn't fair! Paddy hit him when he was down! You should of stopped the fight, Bill.'

'Dinny's right,' declared Charles. 'Aidan didn't have a chance. So Paddy needn't think he was the winner.'

'I won all right,' growled Paddy. 'He ran away, didn't he?'

'I expect he's used to people who fight fairly,' said Charles cuttingly. 'I'd like to take you on myself, Paddy—want to try?'

Paddy pretended not to hear him, for Charles was the best fighter in the Barley Creek school.

'Don't be silly, Charles,' said Harriet. 'It was Aidan's fight, not yours. I'm sure he'll finish it some other time. Come on, Polly—we must go home.'

They filed up the hill through the bluegums and she-oaks and soldier-vines, following the thread of a track that Dinny had shown to Harriet. Polly would have dearly loved to discuss Aidan's behaviour, but Harriet and Rose-Ann refused to open the subject.

'Oh, well, Dinny was quite right—it wasn't a bit fair,' Polly said at last, as they climbed through the fence beside the cowshed. 'That nasty Paddy didn't win, and that's something to be thankful for.'

But Harriet did not break her glum silence. She knew that Polly's remark could never comfort Aidan, nor convince him that he was anything but a coward.

Neither Harriet nor Rose-Ann was surprised to learn at tea-time that Aidan had a headache and was lying down in his room. As soon as the meal was over, Harriet crept along the veranda to the dark little slit of a bedroom at the end. Her knock being unanswered, she pushed open the door.

'It's only me, Harriet,' she ventured, peering through the gloom towards the bed in the corner.

'I don't want to see anyone,' came the ungracious reply.

'Wouldn't you like to hear what the others said?' asked Harriet. 'Everyone thought it wasn't fair, and—'

Aidan sat up, angry and dishevelled.

'What does it matter what they said? It's what I *did* that counts. I ran away—you saw me.'

Harriet, in her desire to comfort him, went too far.

'It seemed such a good idea, this fight. It might have made such a difference.'

'A difference to what?' demanded Aidan, staring at his sister with a sudden understanding. 'You mean you arranged it all, so I would beat Paddy? That's what you were trying to tell me this morning, wasn't it?'

He leapt off the bed with such a threatening air that Harriet backed towards the door.

'You'll meddle in other people's affairs once too often, Harriet! It was a rotten idea, and even if I'd won I would never have come to like this place, or that wretched school, or anyone in it. Now please go away!'

Harriet could do nothing but obey. It was a new experience to be frightened of one's own brother, especially for Harriet, who was so rarely frightened. She fled to the shelter of the sitting-room, where she remained until bedtime, looking so meek and quiet that her mother inquired anxiously after her health.

Despite her unhappiness, and her despondent feeling that she had made matters very much worse for Aidan instead of better, she slept with her usual soundness. It was with some alarm and astonishment that she awoke before sunrise, roused by a loud knocking on the french window.

'Harriet! Get up!' Polly's voice called with a strange urgency. 'Come quick!'

Barefoot, tousle-headed, and certain that she must still be dreaming, Harriet crossed the room and opened the shutters.

'Whatever is it, Polly? It's too early to get up.'

'It's Aidan—his bed ain't hardly been slept in, and we can't find him anywhere. Your father wants to see you—he's in the dining-room. Here—I'll help you dress.'

With Polly's aid, the usually slow process took only a few moments, during which Polly kept up a lively flow of talk.

'Such a turn it gave me! I went in to see if he wanted a cuppa tea, after his headache and all, and there was his bed all empty and him nowhere around.

Nothing much gone, either—only his jacket and cap, and a couple of books. Dunno if he even took any money. Wherever do you suppose he's gone off to? It's real good country here to get lost in, and he don't know his way, any more than a baby would.'

Harriet was too bewildered to reply. Only too thoroughly awake now, she followed Polly round the veranda to the hall and the little dining-room, which was also her father's study. Mr Wilmot sat at his heavy mahogany desk, staring at what Harriet later discovered was a rough map of the Blackhill district.

'Tell Boz to harness the horse immediately,' he said to Polly. 'And then you can go down to the Rectory with a message. I'll write it out for you. Now, Harriet—perhaps you can help me.'

'I don't know where Aidan has gone,' said Harriet. 'I wish I did.'

'If you could tell me *why* he's disappeared, that might help,' said her father. 'I've had a rather muddled version from Polly—something about a fight.'

There was nothing for it but to tell the whole story. Well aware that her own part in it did not sound too noble, Harriet gave the account as rapidly as she could, and then stood gazing at the first, mellow rays of sunlight gilding the tip of the willow tree.

'I see,' said Mr Wilmot. 'So you thought it best to arrange Aidan's affairs for him. I've no doubt your intentions were good, Harriet, but I do wish you would think more and learn to leave well alone. Aidan must have felt too miserable last night to face up to school again this morning. And we have no notion of where he has gone. Did he have any close friends at school at all?'

'No,' said Harriet. 'He didn't talk to anyone, except Mr Burnie.'

'Burnie might be able to help,' reflected Mr Wilmot, speaking to himself rather than to Harriet, who stood before him feeling singularly useless and despondent. She blamed herself entirely for Aidan's disappearance, and would have gladly offered to run straight off into the bush to search for him.

'And please, Harriet,' said her father, as if reading her mind, 'do not try to find your brother. This is work for men, not for little girls. The best thing for you to do is to go and sit with your poor mother.'

Dismissed, Harriet crept away to her mother's room. From the front window she watched Boz and her father drive past the garden and down the track towards the ford. Apparently they were going to search along the Blackhill road—that would be the obvious route for Aidan to choose. But he might already have been gone for some hours, and could have branched off the road in any direction. Harriet gazed across the garden at the stubby, crouching hills beyond the creek, hills that for mile upon mile looked exactly like one another, and had a very poor and scanty welcome to offer to any traveller. Aidan would soon be lost among them.

'Oh, why did we ever come to this horrible place?' cried her mother. 'As soon as Aidan is found, we shall all go back to England immediately.'

Harriet seemed to be defeated at last. She could not fight the entire family, if they decided to leave Lillipilly Hill once Aidan returned to their midst. And if Aidan did not return—but Harriet went on staring at the hills, refusing to follow that train of thought.

7

Aidan meets a Bunyip

Aidan had wakened suddenly at midnight, to find that his headache was worse. At first he stayed in his bed, turning from side to side in a vain effort to recover the lost comfort of sleep. Finally he rose and went to the one small window, which overlooked the eastern garden.

As he stood there, gratefully feeling the fresh, night air on his hot face, the moon swung up over the orchard hill, and shone into his eyes. It was a rather elderly moon, a little lop-sided, but still radiant enough to give life and shape to every bush and tree in the tangled garden. Aidan looked and listened, and could hear tiny sounds—the rustle of grass as a bandicoot padded by, the chirp of crickets, the thud of a possum dropping on to the cowshed roof, and, loneliest of all night noises, the baying of a dog far away down the gully.

He was never quite sure what made him turn back into his room and put on his everyday clothes. Perhaps it was the realization that there was another world beyond the one he knew here—the hated world of school and Paddy Tolly, and the fight that wasn't a fight. By the time he had collected two of his favourite books, and put on his cap, his decision was made. He would leave this unsatisfactory world behind him, and find another.

'If I follow the creek,' he reflected, 'I must reach Blackhill Bay in the end. And the packets go from there to Sydney. I shall have just enough money for my passage. In Sydney I shall surely find some sort of work.'

All the money he had was a half-crown, which he had been keeping in the hope of buying a new book during his next visit to Sydney. Whether it would pay for his journey on the packet he did not know, but in his new and unusual mood of recklessness he did not wait to think about it. He set off hurriedly and silently along the path to the orchard, suddenly vastly exhilarated, and already beginning to forget the bitter experiences of the afternoon.

Aidan's knowledge of local geography was of the scantiest. He had once studied his father's map of the district, and the one fact that he clearly recalled was that Barley Creek flowed into Blackhill Bay. On the map, the distance between Barley Creek township and the bay had not seemed great, but Aidan had to admit that the map was far from accurate. Nor could he remember if any sort of road was marked along the course of the creek.

'It doesn't matter, anyway,' he told himself, as he took a diagonal path across the orchard towards the creek. 'All I need to do is keep to the bank.'

At first it was fairly simple. East of the ford, the creek was quite broad, and the moonlight gleaming on the water gave Aidan enough guidance for him to see and follow a ragged track along the bank. He looked back once, and saw above the orchard the iron roofs of Lillipilly Hill, washed over with silver. Then a line of tall gums hid the house from view, and Aidan was alone with his thoughts, his determination, and his ambition to be as far away as possible before sunrise.

For two or three miles he plodded on, resolutely ignoring the calls of unknown night-birds, and the mysterious crackling of twigs in the scrub, or the occasional splashes in the shadows at the edge of the creek. It occurred to him that if Harriet had been there, she would have been delighted with all these noises, and would have investigated them all. But Aidan's curiosity was not sufficient to outweigh his new resolve, and he kept up his steady pace, hands thrust into his pockets, his books buttoned inside his jacket, his head bent to watch the track, which was becoming more and more overgrown. Soldier-vine and lantana pressed close to the bank, and at times forced Aidan to pick his way gingerly across the stones jutting from the margin of the creek.

He had in his pocket the sturdy, gun-metal watch which his father had given to him on his birthday. He pulled it out and studied it when he at last reached an open space.

'Half past one,' he said to himself, after prolonged peering at the watch-face, tilted towards the moon. 'I must have come about four miles. It can't be much farther.'

He looked around him. Ahead, the creek curved to the left, still broad and placid and slow. The black shape of a hill, rising abruptly from the very edge of the path, effectively blocked any view, while the opposite bank was so densely clothed in scrub as to appear a solid, impenetrable mass.

'No clouds, thank goodness,' observed Aidan, staring up at the star-sprinkled sky. 'I'd better keep going.'

He was feeling rather lonely now. He had not realized how utterly deserted this countryside was—he felt that he might go on walking thus for ever, without meeting another human being.

He had followed the curve of the bank without noticing it, and now he stopped suddenly, seeing nothing but dark water where he had been about to tread. Incredulously, he gazed out over a landscape utterly different from that which he had left a few moments ago. Before him lay a vast swamp, acres of moonlit wasteland dotted with mangroves and clumps of reeds, and apparently limitless. He could not see far enough to discern its farthest boundary—whether it was the bay, or more scrub, or even the sea. Nothing stirred between him and the horizon, and the only sound was the sad cry of a curlew, left behind when others of its kind had migrated northward.

Aidan sat down on a rock, and tried desperately to recall the details of the map. He could not remember hearing a swamp mentioned, but then he had to admit that he had not been sufficiently interested in the district to seek information about it. How he wished now that he had listened to the talk of his schoolfellows! They must surely have known of this place.

So obsessed had he become with the idea of escape

from Barley Creek, that he refused to think of turning back.

'But how can I get across?' he wondered. 'It would be hard enough in daylight, let alone in the middle of the night.'

Aidan was not particularly nervous, nor given to wild fancies, yet the utter desolation and loneliness of this spot began to worry him. City-bred, accustomed always to company, he was now abruptly aware that he could rely on no one but himself for a way out of his predicament. If he remained here to starve, he would probably not be found for days.

A long-drawn howl shattered the quiet of the swamp, and Aidan sat frozen with horror. No bird could ever have made a sound like that. Suddenly Aidan remembered Charles's talk of the bunyip that lived on Maloney's Hill, the mysterious creature that howled in the night.

Cautiously, he turned his head to look back at the hill. It was steeper and rockier than any of its neighbours, and frowned over the swamp like a fierce guardian. It would have made a fitting home for any number of bunyips.

'There are no such things as bunyips,' Aidan told himself firmly. 'It could have been something else—a dog, perhaps.'

Aidan might have been cowed by the sight of blood, and the thought of physical pain, but he was not to be vanquished by such things as unearthly howls and tales of mythical creatures. There might or might not be bunyips—this was a surprising country, where all sorts of fantastic things seemed possible—but this was a situation where one ought to sit quietly and use one's powers of reasoning. Which was just what Aidan did.

'If it was a dog,' he reflected, 'then it's either lost, or it belongs to someone. And if it belongs to someone, there must be a house not far away. If there's a house, then I could ask the way to Blackhill. I'll see if I can find the house, and wait near it till daybreak.'

It seemed a sensible plan. It was almost a relief to hear the howl again—and this time Aidan was certain that it was the baying of a dog. It came from the hillside, immediately above him. Without giving himself further time to think Aidan began to scramble upwards over the jutting rocks, tearing his hands and clothes on the vines and the razor-edged sword-grass, and colliding occasionally with saplings that were invisible here, where the moonlight could not penetrate. The noise of his progress was so great that he did not hear the dog approaching down the slope, and did not see it until it was poised on top of the very rock over which he was climbing.

All this time Aidan had been thinking of dogs as friendly animals. It therefore came as a shock to him to realize that the creature towering above him was most definitely hostile. It was a large dog, and to Aidan it seemed as large as a tiger, with the same bared fangs and gleaming eyes. It stood in a patch of moonlight—looking around frantically, Aidan saw that the nearest tree was some yards away.

The dog growled, and crouched as if ready to spring. Not daring to move, Aidan clung to his rock, staring as if mesmerized into the animal's ugly face.

Another shape detached itself from the shadows under the trees, and came forward to join the dog. As if in a dream—or rather, a nightmare—Aidan found himself gazing up into the muzzle of a rifle, whose barrel gleamed in the moonlight. Holding the rifle was a tall figure that seemed no more friendly than the dog.

Aidan summoned what dignity he could.

'Please call off your dog,' he said. 'I'm not doing any harm.'

'What are you doing here, then?' demanded a suspicious voice. The rifle remained steady in its owner's hand.

'Put down your gun, and I'll tell you,' said Aidan. He began to move upwards, and at once the dog snarled and snapped.

'Down, Patchy,' said the voice, which was quite young and fresh, and belonged, Aidan suspected, to someone not much older than himself. The rifle was slowly lowered, and Aidan was permitted to climb the rock and stand beside the stranger.

'I'm lost, that's all,' said Aidan. 'I'm going to Blackhill.'

He was still shaking from the encounter, and his voice was tremulous, but he hoped that Patchy's owner would put this down to breathlessness.

'Queer time to be going to Blackhill, ain't it? Where did you come from?'

'Barley Creek,' said Aidan shortly.

The other boy stood deep in thought for a few moments.

'I reckon you'd better come home with me,' he said at last, in a more friendly tone. 'You'd never get across the swamp at night. Come on—don't mind Patchy. She won't hurt you unless I tell her to.'

Bewildered and weary, Aidan stumbled up the hill, struggling to keep close behind the stranger, who travelled with the easy confidence of one who knows every yard of the way. It seemed to Aidan that the crest of the hill was quite unattainable—no matter how fast they walked, it never appeared to be any nearer.

Suddenly the dog bounded ahead, with a series

of strangled barks which were her sole expression of pleasure. She vanished into dense undergrowth, and her owner said to Aidan, over his shoulder: 'Watch these vines—they scratch. It's easiest if you get down and crawl.'

He dived after Patchy, and Aidan, feeling that nothing would ever surprise him again after the events of this night, obediently wormed his way through a tunnel of scrub, smelling pungently of damp earth and gum leaves. Standing erect at last, he felt beneath his jacket to reassure himself that his precious books were still safe, and looked about him.

'Here we are—this is my place,' said the boy, not without pride.

Aidan gazed in vain around the clearing just below the top of the hill. There was no sign of a house, or a building of any kind. Before him, a single gigantic bluegum reared against the sky; on one side was a wall of rock, and on the other, a row of scrub pines. He looked at the stranger questioningly.

'Do you live in a tree, then?' he asked, wondering if this could be some strange sort of a joke.

The boy merely gestured towards the rock, and Aidan moved closer. He saw then that the rock was not solid at all, but was in fact a large cave, the entrance being partly hidden by a clump of wattle.

'I'll light the candles,' said the boy, stepping into his domain. 'I let the fire go out at nights, in the summer.'

The squat, tallow candles threw long flickering shadows over the walls of the cave, revealing a level, sandy floor, a bed of bracken and sacking, a battered kettle and frying-pan, a few other eating utensils, and, in the farthest corner, a pile of rabbit skins. Patchy had settled herself in what was obviously her usual position—just inside the entrance. She put her long grey muzzle down on her paws, but her eyes remained open, their gaze fixed steadily upon Aidan.

'Want a drink of tea?' asked the boy, pulling off an ancient felt hat of doubtful shape. He was thin-faced, sunburnt, and black-haired; his eyes were large and very dark. His clothing consisted of a grey undershirt with a spotted handkerchief at the neck, and an old pair of trousers reaching half-way between his knees and his bare feet.

'Yes, please,' said Aidan eagerly, trying not to gape at his host's unusual appearance. After all, he told himself, *he* must look rather strange too, with his clothes torn and stained, and his face still swollen from Paddy's attack—but how extremely remote and senseless that affair seemed now! With a feeling of deep relief and thankfulness he sat on the powdery sand, watching the boy kindling a fire at the stone fireplace beside the wattles.

'My name's Aidan Wilmot. What's yours?'

'Clay,' said the boy, not looking up from his work. Already the pile of dry twigs and bark had begun to catch alight.

'Just Clay? Is that your first or last name?'

'It's the only part that matters,' retorted the boy, and Aidan knew better than to question his host further on the subject, although he was filled with curiosity. Studying Clay covertly, he decided that he could not be more than sixteen. His speech, though it was rough enough, was a little too careful to be that of a swaggie, as far as Aidan could judge.

Aidan transferred his attention to the dog. He had never seen an animal like Patchy before. She was lean but powerfully built, with heavy, muscular forequarters and a large, well-shaped head. In colour she was an odd mottled grey.

'What kind of a dog is she?' asked Aidan.

'Blue cattle-dog, mostly,' said Clay, looking up at last. He hung a billy-can over the fire, and sat down beside Patchy, rubbing the dog's short, wiry hair. 'Best dog there is. She don't like strangers, but she'd do anything for me.'

He was boasting now, about what was obviously

his dearest possession. He glanced at Aidan over Patchy's alert head.

'If I hadn't called her off, Patchy would of kept you there on that rock for hours. She heard you coming— we're not used to having people on the hill, 'specially at night.'

'Is this Maloney's Hill?' demanded Aidan, not wishing to dwell on the subject of his meeting with Patchy.

'Yes—do you mean to say you live in Barley Creek, and don't know Maloney's Hill?'

'We haven't been here long,' said Aidan.

'It's easy to see *that*. Wilmot—wasn't there an old man called Wilmot on Lillipilly Hill?'

'He was my father's uncle. Now my father lives there. Only we might be going back to London soon.'

Clay looked puzzled.

'I thought you said you were on your way to Blackhill?'

So Aidan told him the whole story, beginning with the fight, and not omitting any of the details of his inglorious part in it. Clay listened attentively, without interrupting.

'So I was on my way to Blackhill when I heard your dog, only I thought it might have been a bunyip,' Aidan concluded.

Clay stared at him so fixedly and thoughtfully that Aidan felt uncomfortable, and began to wish that he had not told the other boy about the fight.

'But you weren't scared of walking all the way to Blackhill at night,' Clay said at last. 'Why should you run away from a bit of a punch on the nose?'

'I don't know,' mumbled Aidan. 'Is the tea ready?'

Clay rose and busied himself at the fire. Aidan addressed his back.

'I suppose nothing frightens you. You look as if you could fight anyone.'

Clay handed him a pitch-black, steaming mug of tea. There was no sugar, but it was still the best drink Aidan had ever had.

'I've been in a few fights, over in Blackhill,' said Clay, not boasting now, but frowning in his effort to express his thoughts. 'I just felt real angry, nothing else. I reckon, though, that I'd run a mile if I heard a bunyip in the middle of the night.'

'Do you think there are such things as bunyips, then?' asked Aidan, in surprise.

Clay gazed out at the black and silver hill-top.

'I dunno. Never saw one, but my Pa did. He hadn't been drinking then, either—not that time.'

'Where's your father now?' Aidan had not intended to pry, but his curiosity was getting the better of him. In his experience, boys of sixteen simply did not live entirely on their own, in caves on lonely hill-sides.

'Couldn't tell you,' said Clay indifferently. 'Outback, maybe, with his swag. Haven't seen him for about five years. I don't think Ma knows, either—she works in Blackhill, in the hotel.'

He turned to look directly at Aidan. His eyes were very big and black in the firelight, and quite fierce.

'You're not to tell anyone about me—not anyone. If you do, I'll find out somehow, and come and knock you down.'

Hurt by this attack, Aidan put down his mug.

'I must be going, if you would tell me the way.'

Patchy began to growl, and Clay stepped forward to take Aidan's mug.

'Don't be stupid. I'll get some more tea. You can't leave till daylight, anyway. That's Heron Swamp, and it's five miles wide. Even if I take you, it'll be a whole morning's journey.'

Aidan hesitated, then sat down again. He realized that Clay would make no further apology for his brusqueness, and he found that he did not really mind. The cave was snug and peaceful and safe, and Aidan certainly had no objection to staying there until dawn. His determination to reach Blackhill had become dulled and weakened; he just wanted to sit near Clay's fire, drinking tea and talking.

'You must know the district very well,' he said, carefully avoiding asking questions. 'I had no idea that swamp was there.'

'I could find my way across in my sleep, now,' said Clay. 'But it's dangerous for people who don't know it. That's why we're waiting till it's light.'

'You don't have to come with me,' said Aidan. 'If you just point out the path—'

'There ain't just one path,' said Clay, with exaggerated patience. 'There's about a dozen, and you have to know them all. Part of that swamp is so deep you'd sink in half a minute. Anyhow, I've got to go into Blackhill with some skins—it might as well be tomorrow. I need more flour and tea and stuff, too.'

'Are there many rabbits here?' asked Aidan vaguely.

'Plenty, if you know where to hunt. There's fish in the creek, too, and wild duck on the swamp. I don't starve, if that's what you mean. I grow my own potatoes, and make my own damper. When the fire dies down I'll show you how.'

'I wouldn't know how to begin, if I lived up here like you,' said Aidan humbly.

'It comes easy to me,' said Clay, with a return of his former boastfulness. 'My grandpa was an abo—

king of the tribe, Ma reckons. He lived off the country all his life. I take after him.'

He broke off and glanced at Aidan suspiciously.

'I ain't talked as much for years. Mostly I just talk to Patchy.'

'I swear I won't tell a soul about you, or anything you've said,' promised Aidan.

'All right, I believe you,' muttered Clay. 'But why don't you talk, for a change? What about that steamship you came to Sydney in? Is it bigger than the packets that go from Blackhill?'

So Aidan told him of the journey from London, and the storms at sea, and the crossing of the Bight. He told him, too, about the Wilmots' home in London, and his old school, and even about Harriet and Rose-Ann. To all of this Clay listened open-mouthed and wide-eyed.

'You mean you like school, and reading, and all that?'

'Yes,' admitted Aidan. 'I brought two books with me—see?'

Clay stared in astonishment at the two volumes.

'What did you bring those for? You should of brought a water-bag, and a gun. You're like my Pa—he always had a book in his pocket. He didn't have no sense, either. I never read anything in my life—I didn't stay at school more'n a week.'

'Your father must have gone to school, though,' Aidan said.

'Oh, yes, he went to some place back in England or somewhere. He talked like you, real high-falutin'. I dunno what he'd think of me,' said Clay, in genuine wonderment.

Aidan took off his jacket and folded it to make a pillow. He would never have believed that he could have been so comfortable, stretched out on the bare, sandy ground. Presently he dozed, and Clay sat on by the fire, as if keeping watch.

Aidan awoke to find the cave lit by something more than the glow of the fire. He groped for his watch, and discovered that it was a quarter to six. Already the trees outside had definite shapes and colours, and the sky was a creamy shade, soft and pure.

Clay knelt by the fire, raking away the ashes. As Aidan watched, Clay, with the aid of two sticks, drew from the fire a round, blackened object which he carefully set on a piece of bark to cool. Looking round, he saw Aidan gazing at him, and grinned.

'This is your breakfast—come and see.'

Aidan peered at the object, which Clay was cutting with his pocket-knife. Inside, it was white and doughy.

'Damper,' said Clay briefly. 'Have some.'

It was still steaming, and the outside had a distinctly smoky flavour, but it was certainly satisfying, and Aidan was far too hungry to be critical. He and Clay ate in silence, until nothing remained of the damper but a rather meagre portion for Patchy, who sat hopefully between the boys, watching every mouthful.

'I was going to give you a bit for your dinner,' said Clay. 'But I reckon you'll just have to make do with a bit of old biscuit. That's all I've got left. We should be in Blackhill before midday, anyhow. Come on.'

He threw sand on the dying fire, picked up his pile of skins and his gun, and was off, followed by the eager Patchy. Aidan stopped to look rather wistfully back at the cave, and the sentinel gum, before he too crawled into the tunnel.

As they clambered down the hill-side, the full immensity of the swamp became apparent. Reed-beds and mangrove clumps were dark patches on a silver-grey inland sea. A faint line at the edge of the sky marked the lagoon where the swamp finally met the shore. For a moment, half-way down the hill, Aidan stood still. Clay and Patchy progressed with such practised quietness that they were hardly audible, and the only sound in all that wilderness was the gentle lapping of water upon rocks and mud-flats.

With a growing feeling of excitement, Aidan saw the shining disk of the sun sliding up over the horizon, and the surface of the swamp changing to palest pink. The first rays of the sun caught a pair of birds, poised on a half-sunken log—they were tall, long-necked, graceful as resting dancers, and snowy-white.

Aidan hurried after Clay, who plunged ahead without a glance at the scene before him.

'Those birds,' said Aidan, pointing over the swamp. 'What are they?'

'They're white cranes,' said Clay. 'You see a lot of them on the swamp. Those other ones, the black ones, are shags, and there are dozens of herons. You can't eat them, though.' ·

'Eat them!' repeated Aidan in horror. 'That's the last thing I'd want to do! They're beautiful.'

Clay stared at him in amazement.

'Well, even if they are, we haven't got time to stand here looking at them. It's getting late.'

They emerged on to the rocks at the edge of the swamp. The cranes, startled by their approach, rose into the air and flapped clumsily away, no longer graceful, but still lovely to watch, with the sunlight glinting on their wings. All over the swamp darker shapes rose up against the sky, and the herons rent the silence with their indignant croaks.

127

Aidan turned to look at the creek, and the track he had followed the night before, and knew that he could not go with Clay.

'I'm going home, after all,' he said. 'I want to stay.'

Clay merely tipped his elderly hat forward and scratched the back of his head.

'Make up your mind, then. I've got things to do.'

Aidan held out his hand.

'Thank you for the tea and the damper and everything. And I won't tell.'

Clay shook the proffered hand in some embarrassment, and whistled to the dog.

'Come on, Patchy. And watch where you're going—no chasing birds.'

'Perhaps I might see you again later on,' suggested Aidan, not very hopefully.

'I know where to find you if I want to,' said Clay, over his shoulder. He stepped lightly from one clump of grass to the next, not looking back, and soon he was well out on the swamp, with Patchy close behind him, the only objects moving now between Aidan and the horizon.

Clay had not asked the reason for Aidan's decision—and had he done so, Aidan would have found it difficult to give him an answer. Clay would never have understood if Aidan had told him that a sunrise and a pair of white cranes had had something to do with it. For the first time Aidan had seen the beauty of his new country, and could begin to realize why Harriet loved it so much.

But it needed more than that to shake Aidan's resolve. He had left Lillipilly Hill because he had shown himself a coward to his school-mates—that did not matter now. What he wanted was to prove to Clay, not to the others, that he still had courage. And the way to prove it, he reasoned, was not to go on to Blackhill, which would have meant he was running away once again, but to return to Barley Creek and the school, and face the taunts and jeers.

'That's what Clay would do himself,' reflected Aidan. 'Only he would never have given up the fight in the first place.'

He might not meet Clay again. He knew too little about him to be certain that he could always be found on Maloney's Hill. He and Patchy together might vanish like a dream, and Aidan would not have been surprised. But Clay was his friend, and as long as the Wilmots remained on Lillipilly Hill, there was a chance of renewing that friendship.

Thus it was that Harriet, standing at her mother's window, feeling guilty and fearful and altogether miserable, could hardly believe her eyes when she saw her brother climb through the orchard sliprail. After she had spread the glad news, and rushed to meet him, she suddenly realized that Aidan looked oddly different. It was not just that his clothes were torn and dirty, and his eyes shadowy from weariness. He walked with a new confidence, as if he had never heard of Paddy Tolly, or fighting, or punched noses.

The inevitable question burst from the excited Harriet.

'Wherever have you been?'

'I've been to Maloney's Hill, and seen where the bunyip lives,' replied Aidan calmly. 'Has everyone gone out to look for me?'

'Father and Boz are out in the buggy,' said Harriet. 'But Mother has sent Polly to the Rectory to ask Charles to go after them. Charles has a pony—did you know? Did you *see* the bunyip? What did it look like?'

'No, I didn't see it. I only saw its cave. And there's a swamp, Harriet, an enormous one, and hundreds of birds—'

'Will you take me there one day?' asked Harriet wistfully. 'I know I don't deserve it, after helping Charles arrange the fight, but I really did think it was the best thing to do.'

'It doesn't matter now,' said Aidan. 'But next time I'll pick my own fights, thank you.'

'I expect Mother's got your breakfast ready,' said Harriet, relieved to let the subject drop. 'You must be hungry.'

'No, I'm not,' said Aidan dreamily. 'I've had breakfast.'

Aidan apologized to his father for the trouble he had caused, was readily forgiven, and returned to school that afternoon. The others stared, whispered, and one or two sneered, but Aidan ignored them all until lessons were finished. Then he walked up to Paddy Tolly.

'If you want another fight, then just tell me the time and the place. I promise you I won't run away this time—if you promise to fight fair.'

Thoroughly flustered, Paddy looked to his little band of followers for support. At last the smallest, one of the urchins from the second form, spoke up: 'What d'you want to fight 'im *for*, Paddy? 'E never did anything to you, did 'e?'

'That's right, he didn't,' broke in Dinny. 'Why don't you forget about the bloomin' fight? Charley Farmer wants us all for cricket practice—don't forget, he's playing against Deacon's Flat on Sat'dee.'

And Aidan, allowed the privilege of bowling the first ball to Charles—a doubtful privilege, for Charles drove it right outside the school grounds—heard no more of fights. The coming cricket match was of much greater importance.

8

The Cricket Match

On Friday Harriet set about persuading her father to take all three children to Deacon's Flat on the following day. Always extremely alert to what was happening around her, Harriet had succumbed to the cricket fever at present raging in the Barley Creek school, although she had never watched a game of cricket in her life.

'You see, Father,' she said earnestly, having followed Mr Wilmot to the orchard sliprail after tea, 'this is the most important match of the year. It's the last, and whoever wins get a—what do you call it?—a sort of prize, only it's just to look at—'

'Trophy,' suggested her father, puffing serenely

at his pipe, and gazing over the orchard towards the mauve and misty hills.

'That's it, a trophy, and Deacon's Flat have won it for the last three years, only this year Barley Creek have a much stronger team, Charles says. Joe O'Brien's to be playing, and he's the best bat in the district.'

'All this is very interesting, Harriet,' observed Mr Wilmot. 'You seem to have been studying the game. Am I to understand that you would like to go and watch this contest tomorrow?'

Harriet peered up at him sideways in an unsuccessful attempt to discover if he were smiling. Pipe and beard combined to hide his expression.

'Don't you think we should, Father? If we are to live here, then we should be interested in the things the Barley Creek people do, shouldn't we?'

To her relief, her father laughed.

'You needn't sound so smug, Harriet. Very well, let's assume we are to stay at Lillipilly Hill, and support the Barley Creek cricket team. Have you decided how we are to travel to Deacon's Flat?'

'Oh, that's quite easy,' said Harriet cheerfully. 'Charles will ride his pony, and that will leave room in the Farmers' buggy for Rose-Ann and me, if we squeeze. Then Boz can take you and Aidan.'

Her father stared at her in unwilling admiration.

'There's no doubt, Harriet, that you have a genius for interference.'

'Yes, Father,' murmured Harriet, uncertain whether this was a reproof or a joke. After all, this could hardly be called meddling, not the sort of meddling that had led to Aidan's disappearance. She waited.

'You have overlooked just one thing,' said Mr Wilmot. 'Your mother and I have already discussed this match, and decided to go. It will be an outing for your mother, and she has had few enough since we came here.'

Harriet thought for a moment.

'Well, perhaps Aidan could ride behind Charles on the pony—it's quite a strong pony, and when it got tired, Aidan could walk for a bit. Charles will have to ride, because of keeping his strength for the cricket—'

'It won't be necessary for the poor animal to carry a double load,' said Mr Wilmot. 'As a matter of fact, Boz is staying behind, and I'm driving the buggy. That will leave room for Aidan.'

Harriet's thin, freckled face glowed with excitement.

'Oh, Father, what a good idea for all of us to go! And do you know, they're making Aidan twelfth man, because there isn't anyone else. Won't it be wonderful if he plays?'

'Aidan might not think so,' said Mr Wilmot. 'He was never in the school team, was he?'

'No,' admitted Harriet. 'But Charles has been coaching him. Does Polly know about the tea? We must take plenty to eat, because the match lasts all afternoon, and we shan't be home before dark.'

'I am sure Polly knows the arrangements,' said Mr Wilmot. 'And in view of all the excitement, Harriet, shouldn't you go early to bed?'

Harriet went off obediently towards the house, leaving her father in dreamy contemplation of the orchard, seeing in place of the straggling peach and apple trees orderly rows of orange and lemon, which he hoped to plant in the spring.

The day of the great match was gratifyingly warm and sunny, with a brisk wind blowing from the sea, and a few high, snow-white clouds marching across the sky. Harriet spent the morning bowling to Aidan at the top of the cow-paddock.

'Perhaps it's as well,' she sighed at last, 'that you won't be playing. I've bowled you at least ten times, and I'm the worst bowler in the world. You've only hit about three balls.'

Aidan was quite unperturbed. He put on his jacket and strolled off to dinner, secure in the knowledge that Barley Creek could field eleven strong men and boys in the best of health, and that his services were not at all likely to be required.

The Barley Creek supporters turned out in full force, assembling in a noisy and cheerful group outside Mrs Tolly's store. A dray drawn by four stolid cart-horses was to carry the heroes of the hour, the members of the eleven—except for Charles, who preferred his pony. The cricketers had attired themselves in flannels ranging in shade from pale grey to rich cream, shirts to match, and an odd and colourful assortment of caps. Bright blue sashes were to be their distinguishing marks, and these they wore about their waists. Harriet stared in awed admiration at the team as she and Rose-Ann were escorted by Polly up the hill to the Rectory.

'Which is Joe O'Brien?' Harriet whispered to Polly.

'Surely you can pick *him*,' said Polly. 'He's like all the O'Briens—skinny, with a lot of black hair. That's him, just getting on the dray. One of the wildest boys they ever had in Barley Creek, but they do say he's a wonderful bat.'

Indeed, the boy Polly indicated was an older, masculine edition of Dinny, who was now scrambling up behind her brother.

'The cheek of 'er,' said Polly indignantly. 'That dray's supposed to be for the team. Trust an O'Brien to push its way in.'

But Harriet was pleased that Dinny was to be at the match, and secretly a little envious, for the dray looked a much more exciting mode of transport than the decorous buggy belonging to the Rectory. However, she was consoled by being allowed to sit on the floor, with her legs dangling over the side, while Rose-Ann was wedged on to the seat between the minister and his wife.

'I hope you're comfortable, Harriet,' said Mrs Farmer anxiously. 'Do hold on tight, won't you?'

Harriet promised that she would, and the Rectory horse, a much younger and more skittish animal than Barrel, started off down the hill in fine style, with Charles following.

'I understand we're to lead the procession,' said Mr Farmer. 'We seem to have the fastest turn-out. There's a heavy load on that dray.'

Looking back as they approached the O'Briens' cottage, Harriet could see the cart-horses lumbering valiantly up the hill, and behind them some five or six buggies, including the Wilmots', the Tollys', and the Mackenzies'. Mrs O'Brien stood at the door to watch them pass, and the younger O'Brien children lined the roadside in a disconsolate row, not having been as fortunate—or as daring—as Dinny.

'Mind you hit 'em all for six, Joe!' called

Mrs O'Brien to her son. 'An' don't forget to bring back that trophy!'

This was greeted by loud cheers from the dray, and confident assurances that the trophy would indeed return to Barley Creek. And then the O'Briens' shack was left behind, as the road curved away into the hills—craggy, sharp-faced hills, clothed in coarse grass and bracken, and well populated by rabbits and hares that scuttled to safety at the noise of the cricketers' approach. Once Harriet spied a wallaby loping over the crest of a hill, and farther on a flock of pink and grey galahs rose in shrill protest from their feeding-ground, their rosy breasts bright in the sunlight.

'This is where I hunt rabbits, Harriet,' said Charles, coming up beside the buggy. 'It's the best place for miles around. But I'm not the only one who hunts there now. I saw a fellow over on the edge of the scrub yesterday—he disappeared when he saw me. He had a dog with him—a sort of grey dog, quite big. Do you think it might be the bush-ranger, Father?'

'You shouldn't listen to all this gossip about the bush-ranger,' said Mr Farmer. 'No one knows for sure that there is one, and very little theft has been reported. The person you saw was no doubt simply catching a few rabbits for the family dinner. Goodness knows there are enough rabbits for the taking.'

'When could I come hunting with you, Charles?' asked Harriet hopefully. 'I promise I wouldn't make a noise.'

'My dear Harriet, I'm sure your mother would never allow it,' protested Mrs Farmer. 'Shooting is no sport for girls, and some of the country Charles covers is very rough.'

Harriet sighed resignedly, knowing that this was the answer she might have expected.

'But if you wish, I shall take you and Rose-Ann out one day to look at some of the birds,' said Mr Farmer kindly, for he secretly felt rather sorry for Harriet in her well-ordered and sheltered existence. 'Your mother would not object to that.'

And with this Harriet had to be content.

After about four miles of travel, the road widened, and the hills receded on either side of the level valley that gave Deacon's Flat part of its name. A reedy little creek wound down to join the road, and a few peppercorn trees gave a shade that was now very welcome, for the wind did not blow strongly here, and the afternoon sun flooded the valley with a golden heat.

Charles, who had ridden back to see how the others were faring, suddenly shouted: 'Hurry up, Father, they're getting ready to pass you!'

Harriet, not knowing that it was traditional to race over the last mile into the township, clung in astonishment to her perch as Mr Farmer called a warning and began to urge on the horse.

'Now do be careful, Harry,' said Mrs Farmer—and the remark was also traditional, as well as futile. For Barley Creek's minister was an expert and enthusiastic horseman, and to him this was the great event of the day. The buggy swayed and bumped along the dusty ruts of the road, the horse pricked up its ears delightedly, and Rose-Ann clutched apprehensively at Mrs Farmer as the sound of trotting hooves and creaking wheels filled the air.

'Here comes Mr Burnie!' cried Charles. 'He's passed all the others. Go on, Father!'

The schoolmaster's buggy was indeed approaching at a rapid pace—it was a lighter vehicle than most of the others, and Mr Burnie and his wife were the only occupants. The cricketers, whose own dray was gradually falling right to the rear of the procession, cheered wildly as schoolmaster and minister drew level, with only a quarter of a mile to go.

Harriet, trembling with excitement, and heedless of the fine, white dust settling on her blue gingham dress, uttered a most unladylike sound that could only be described as a yell.

'Look! Father's coming! He's going to pass you, Mr Farmer!'

To everyone's amazement, the Wilmot buggy appeared almost from nowhere to challenge the leaders. Harriet could see her father, who had occasionally driven a gig along English country lanes during his holidays, now handling the buggy reins as confidently as if he had lived all his life in the New South Wales bush. Barrel, greatly astonished, must have remembered something of his honourable past, for he responded as gallantly as any three-year-old. Mrs Wilmot, holding her dainty straw hat with one hand, and the seat with the other, was flushed and laughing, and Aidan was shouting encouragement to his father.

The first house in Deacon's Flat was now only a hundred yards away. Fortunately the road was flanked by broad, grassy verges, and two vehicles were well able to travel abreast. Mr Farmer was obliged at last to fall behind, as Mr Burnie and Francis Wilmot raced together into the township. A Deacon's Flat resident, leaning on his gate and watching the finish, declared that the Wilmot buggy won by about half a yard, and no one was in a position to dispute his judgement.

'The best race we've had in years,' said Mr Farmer, when the horses had finally been halted outside the post office. 'Your father drove splendidly, Harriet.'

Harriet jumped down and ran to pat Barrel, who stood with heaving sides but proudly raised head, in the middle of a group of Deacon's Flat children.

'He's an old 'un to be winning races, ain't he?' said one boy admiringly.

'He's a wonderful horse, even if he is old,' declared Harriet. 'He wanted to show those younger horses how good he still is—didn't you, Barrel?'

'You're new, ain't you?' asked the boy. 'Ain't seen any of you before.'

'We live at Lillipilly Hill,' said Harriet proudly. 'We shall be here next year, too.'

And just then she could well believe her own prophecy. For the first time the Wilmots seemed really to belong to Barley Creek, as the other buggy-owners and the cricketers clustered round to congratulate Mr Wilmot and to rub Barrel's nose.

'Come on,' said the Deacon's Flat boy at last. 'Why don't they start the game? Our team's all ready—and they ain't half keen to keep that there trophy.'

It was then that Harriet realized that Joe O'Brien was not with the rest of the team. She turned to look for him and saw Dinny coming towards her, supporting a limping Joe. Dinny's face was screwed up with anxiety.

'Joe's hurt hisself,' she said. 'He slipped, jumping off the dray. It's his ankle that's bad.'

143

'Then he won't be able to play?' said Harriet in alarm.

Aidan, who had been watching the horses, now gave the unfortunate Joe his whole attention.

'He might be quite fit by the time they start playing,' he suggested without conviction—for Joe had obviously damaged his ankle and could hardly put his right foot to the ground.

'No, he won't,' said Harriet, positively and unkindly. 'So you'll have to take his place. Perhaps they'll declare before it's your turn to bat.'

'But I can't bowl either,' groaned Aidan, and for most of the Barley Creek innings he cast numerous glances at Joe, now resting his badly sprained ankle in the shade. Aidan's own face reflected Joe's gloom.

The entire population of Deacon's Flat— numbering perhaps fifty or sixty—had turned out either to participate in the match or to watch it. The field of battle was the wide, grassy paddock behind the post office, where the spectators could gather along the fence under the gums and turpentines. Mr Wilmot was the only one who had had the foresight to bring cushions for his family—the others sat on the grass, or on the fence railings.

'A perfect setting,' said Mr Wilmot with satisfaction, as he surveyed the pale green paddock, the graceful, silvery trees, and the darker background of the hills. But all other eyes were on the two captains, now entering the field—Steve Jackson, a farmer from Barley Creek, and John Wilkins, known as 'Demon' Wilkins, the Deacon's Flat fast bowler, who away from the cricket pitch was the quietest and mildest of men, the owner of the local dairy. To the delight of the visitors, Steve won the toss, and presently he and Charles came out to open the innings for Barley Creek.

'Do they only play one innings each, then?' Mr Wilmot asked Mr Farmer. 'It's half past one, and we can't have more than four hours of daylight left.'

'It's usually a fast and furious match,' said the minister. 'It's always been a half-day affair, to suit the farmers, who can't afford to be away from their work for long. It has been known, though, for the game to continue by moonlight.'

At first, much to Harriet's delight, it seemed that this might even be another such occasion, for Charles and Steve kept up their partnership for half an hour, making twenty-five runs in defiance of Demon Wilkins and his low, mean ball that some Barley Creek supporters described resentfully as a 'molly-grubber'. And then Steve, in his anxiety to add one more run, slipped and fell between the wickets. By the time he had picked himself up again the wicket keeper had whipped off the bails.

After this disaster the innings did not last long. An hour and a half after commencement of play, Barley Creek was all out for the not very brilliant total of sixty-nine; Aidan, going in ninth, had been out second ball. Charles, who carried his bat and had scored twice as many runs as anyone else, approached his parents with an unusual air of despondency.

'We might as well go home,' he said. 'We can never win now. Just our luck to lose Joe!'

'But you've got Aidan instead,' said Rose-Ann loyally, having grasped this much of the complicated proceedings going on in front of her.

Charles gave her a look which in a less good-natured boy would have been contemptuous.

'Well, yes, we have. Let's have tea.'

Polly had not been frugal in her catering—but then, she never was. And for once Mrs Wilmot did not complain of her servant's extravagance, for the long drive and the fresh air had sharpened all appetites. The postmistress had huge pots of water boiling on her capacious stove—from these the visitors filled their billy-cans to make tea, and the Wilmots drank the strong, black liquid with the rest. Only Harriet ate her chicken sandwiches and jam tarts with unappreciative haste, being anxious for the game to continue.

'Why don't they start?' she lamented. 'It's getting late.'

'I wish it was dark,' said Aidan fervently.

But at last the Barley Creek players began to straggle on to the field, and Aidan was summoned to join them. Steve put him right out on the boundary, where, he hoped, he would not be needed. This cheered Aidan a little, for he had dreaded being placed close to the wicket, in a highly dangerous and conspicuous position.

The Deacon's Flat batsmen were full of confidence, and ready to take risks with the bowling of Charles and Steve. Unluckily, their risks seemed to be justified. The score rose steadily, while the bowlers grew redder and wearier, and the spirits of the Barley Creek supporters sank with the declining sun.

'They'll have to change the bowling soon,' said Mr Farmer. 'It's nearly half past four, and those two openers are still there.'

Charles went up to speak to Steve, who answered him in evident astonishment. Finally he shrugged resignedly, and walked towards Aidan.

'They're going to let him bowl!' cried Harriet.

'I'm afraid,' said Mr Farmer, 'that it's a case of try anything now.'

No player could have been more reluctant than Aidan to take his chance. He approached the wicket with his head down and his hands clasped behind him; he took the ball from Steve as gingerly as if it were a hot coal. Fortunately Charles had coached him sufficiently for him to know where to make his run, and how to move his arm, but any bowling he had done up till now had been of the gentle, schoolgirlish variety. And somehow he felt that the batsman, a huge red-headed fellow who was the Deacon's Flat blacksmith, would not treat such balls with anything but the contempt they deserved.

He was quite right. The blacksmith hit a six off the first ball, and a four off the second. The third went too wide to be even considered. Charles groaned, Harriet shut her eyes, and someone gave a loud laugh. Aidan knew that laugh—it was Paddy Tolly's. The sound of it roused Aidan's anger. He hadn't asked to play in this wretched match, he had never claimed to be a cricketer, and here he was forced into the position he hated most—that of a laughing-stock.

'If I just throw the ball as hard as I can, I can't do any worse,' he told himself. 'And then they're sure to take me off.'

The next minute a great shout went up from the onlookers, as the bails flew, the umpire raised his hand, and the bewildered blacksmith retired to the fence, shaking his head. It would have been hard to say who was the more astonished—batsman or bowler. Aidan stared at the ball now once more reposing in his hand, as if wondering whether it possessed magic powers.

'Go on, Aidan, do it again!' shrieked Harriet, and for once she was not reminded that it was unladylike to shout.

Aidan did his best. The next ball was very short, and the new batsman, thoroughly puzzled, made the mistake of poking forward at it, thus presenting Charles with the easiest of catches.

Amidst cheers, Aidan bowled his fifth ball, which went about a yard wide of the wicket. This time nobody laughed, and Aidan regained his confidence sufficiently to send down a quite respectable straight ball which the batsman played cautiously back to him, without scoring.

Steve very sensibly took Aidan off again, knowing that the boy was perfectly capable of returning to his earlier disastrous form in the next over. But the dismissal of two of Deacon's Flat's best batsmen had inspired the Barley Creek team, and in the next ten minutes three more wickets fell. With the score at five for forty-nine, the Barley Creek supporters began to look quite cheerful, and the Deacon's Flat inhabitants grew steadily quieter and grimmer.

'We might even have them all out by five,' exulted Mr Farmer, consulting his watch. 'There's only one good bat left—that fellow Charles is bowling to now. They call him "Slogger", and it suits him.'

Slogger, a stout, solid young man, chewed thoughtfully on a grass stem as he dispatched a succession of balls to the boundary, or near it. Up and up went the score, and Slogger remained at the wicket, unruffled by the brisk removal of his partner. He seemed as immovable as the rocky hill-side behind him.

'Six for sixty,' groaned Mr Wilmot, who was as thoroughly absorbed in the game as the minister. 'We'll never do it.'

'Aidan's going to bowl again,' said Harriet excitedly. 'Don't you think he's a good bowler, Father? We could still win.'

'With coaching and practice, he might make a bowler,' said Mr Wilmot. 'But at present, he's merely lucky. Let's hope his luck holds.'

Aidan began badly, and Slogger scored an easy two. Aidan walked back very slowly to start his next run, giving himself time to think. He knew little enough about cricket, but he had been watching Slogger for some time, and his critical mind had registered the fact that the Deacon's Flat batsman treated every ball in the same manner—he stepped out boldly, and slashed. So far it had worked beautifully.

'But,' reflected Aidan, 'if he couldn't step out, and went back instead, something different might happen.'

It was a sound theory, and all that remained was to put it into practice. Aidan had very little idea of how to go about it, but in a happy inspiration he aimed directly at Slogger's large boots. Surprised, Slogger stepped back, swung at the ball in his usual enthusiastic fashion, and knocked the bails right off the wicket.

'I am beginning to change my opinion,' remarked Mr Wilmot, when the cheering had subsided. 'Aidan *is* a bowler. He bowls with his head.'

'But Father, how can he?' demanded Rose-Ann, in genuine bewilderment, only to be squashed by Harriet.

'Don't be so stupid, Rose-Ann—Father means Aidan thinks all the time. He's just as clever at cricket as he is at lessons. Oh, I *am* glad Paddy Tolly's here!'

The match was soon finished, once Slogger had been dismissed. At ten past five, Deacon's Flat were all out for sixty-six, and Aidan was chaired to the fence.

'They want you to go out with Steve to take the trophy,' said Charles, beaming with delight at his schoolfellow's success. 'John Wilkins is just bringing it out. Go on, Aidan—you won't have to make a speech.'

Reluctantly, Aidan allowed himself to be pushed to the centre of the field, where he stood self-consciously while the trophy, a huge brass tray engraved with the records of past matches, was ceremoniously handed over to Steve. During John's brief but halting speech, Aidan stared over his head at the hillside, now glowing in the full light of the sinking sun. For an instant, the light glinted on the silver-grey head of a large dog, and the black hair of a boy, crouching behind a rock. Aidan raised his hand in a faint salute, and he was certain that Clay gave an answering wave before both figures melted away into the gilded scrub. It made Aidan's satisfaction complete, and meant more than all the acclamation of the Barley Creek folk, more even than the envious glances of Paddy, and the knowledge that hereafter he would never lack for friends.

The drive home was quiet and sedate, at least in the buggies. From the dray came sounds of singing, but that was far behind, and along the road all the bush creatures were silent, save for an occasional mopoke or frog. The wind had died away at sunset, and on the hill-tops the trees leant motionless against the painted sky. Rose-Ann slept, but Harriet was wide-awake, still excited over the cricket match and reliving every moment of Aidan's triumph. It had been a wonderful day. Surely, after this, there would be much less talk at Lillipilly Hill of returning to London? Aidan would be a hero at school now, instead of an outcast, and if he were happy, then his father and mother would be happier, too. To Harriet, that evening, the whole world was as rosy as the western sky.

> *'Singin' toorali, toorali, addidee,*
> *For we're bound fer Botany Bay.'*

The words echoed down the track, and Harriet whispered them to herself, for Polly had taught her the chorus. It was indeed a time for singing.

9

Journey to the Sea

Harriet was playing scales. At least, she should have been. Actually, one hand strayed over the keyboard while the other groped in her pinafore pocket for the last crumbs of her mid-morning bun. It had been an excellent bun, round and shiny and well endowed with currants, and Harriet was wondering whether it would be advisable to go to the kitchen to ask Polly for another one.

'Is Mother in the kitchen?' she demanded of Rose-Ann, who sat at the window, sewing.

'Yes—it's baking day. You know that.'

'I thought perhaps they'd finished,' said Harriet sadly. If her mother was in the kitchen, then it was no good looking for another bun. An hour's practice every day was the rule for both girls, and it must not be interrupted.

'Is it still raining?' asked Harriet, bringing her empty hand out of her pocket and placing it reluctantly on the keys.

'Not quite so hard,' said Rose-Ann, peering out across the veranda. 'I can see a tiny bit of blue sky.'

'Don't you ever wish very hard that something would happen?' said Harriet, playing a violent discord. 'I do. Nothing has happened for weeks.'

It was the middle of May. The school had closed for the autumn holidays, and Lillipilly Hill was wrapped in what was to Harriet an intolerable quiet. Aidan had gone with his father to Sydney, where Mr Wilmot had some business to transact, and they were to be away for several days. Charles was staying with some relatives in Blackhill, and since the school closed Harriet had seen nothing of Dinny. So Harriet was feeling extremely lonely and bored, and the great day of the cricket match seemed incredibly distant.

'But lots of things have happened,' said the practical Rose-Ann. 'Boz is digging out the apple trees, and the brown cow has had a calf, and Mother sent for the muslin for our new bedroom curtains. And we are to be measured for our winter dresses next week. I'm to have dark blue, with white braid, and yours is to be brown, I think—'

'I hate brown,' said Harriet crossly. 'And that's not what I meant about things happening. Those are just little things. I want something to happen to *me*, like being allowed to go hunting with Charles— only he's not here—or exploring that swamp Aidan saw. We've not been farther than the front gate since school finished.'

'It's too wet, anyway,' said Rose-Ann, who was perfectly content to be snug and safe indoors, with her sewing—she was making the ruffles for the new curtains—and the knowledge that there was no more school for ten days.

Harriet sighed at her sister's lack of perception, and attempted a few more scales. She had just decided to give up the scales and play one of her pieces instead, when the sitting-room door opened, and her mother came in.

'Harriet, dear, I'm afraid I must ask you to run down to the village for me. Polly is very busy, and I want this letter to go by this afternoon's post. I hope you will be all right on your own. Just go straight down and come back as soon as you have given Mr Mackenzie the letter. It's stopped raining, but you had better put on your coat.'

Harriet was in the hall almost before her mother had finished speaking. Never before had she been allowed to go on an errand quite by herself. She dragged on her coat, took the letter, and dived for the front door.

'You can finish your practising when you come back,' Mrs Wilmot called after her, but even that could not make Harriet's excursion any the less welcome. She slithered down the track, over the wet leaves and shining stones, and splashed gaily through the puddles at the bottom.

Harriet loved going to the post office, whither she had often gone with Polly after morning school. It was a dark, cramped little place, stifling in summer and cheerless in winter, but to Harriet it was positively exciting. Mr Mackenzie presided behind a rough wooden counter, in front of a row of pigeon-holes marked in chalk with all the letters of the alphabet. Harriet always looked with particular interest at Q, X, and Z, but today, as usual, they were empty. She had spent some time, generally during music or sewing lessons, inventing names beginning with these letters.

'Good morning, Harriet,' said the postmaster cheerfully. 'Out on your own, are you? Here, you can stamp the letter if you like.'

He pushed over the rusty tin containing the post office stamp, and Harriet carefully imprinted the date and the name, 'Barley Creek'.

'Any mail for us?' she asked, glancing hopefully at W.

'Not yet,' said Mr Mackenzie, without looking, for he knew just which families had received mail by the previous post. 'There might be some when Jock comes this afternoon.'

Harriet could find no further excuse for lingering. She went outside and stared along the road. As if in answer to her wish, Dinny appeared at the doorway of Mrs Tolly's store, carring a bulging sack. Harriet waved joyfully, and they met half-way between the store and the post office.

'I can't stay long,' said Harriet regretfully. 'I came down to post a letter, and I have to go back and finish my practice.'

'You still playing that old piano?' demanded Dinny. 'Not, mind you, that I wouldn't have a try at it instead of digging potatoes—that's real hard work. An' termorrer I've got to go all the way to Winneroo with baccy an' stuff for Pa.'

'How are you to get there?' asked Harriet.

'On my two feet, of course. It's only five mile. Want to come?'

Harriet stared at her friend in astonishment.

'I'd never be allowed.'

'Why not? There's a good track, an' no snakes or nothing. We'd be back before dark, easily. Winneroo's a good place—there's hundreds of shells, an' little pools in the rocks, an' all that sand—'

'I should love to go,' said Harriet wistfully. 'I've not seen the sea since we came here.'

'Oh, well,' said Dinny, 'if you want to come, meet me at our fence at seven o'clock. An' bring some dinner with you. I've got to get back now—Ma's waiting on this bag of stores. She's going to make a treacle pudding—Pa sent us some money last week.'

Harriet trudged back home in a thoughtful mood. To Harriet, few things were impossible. At first, the idea of going to Winneroo with Dinny was just an idle dream. But as she climbed the hill towards the lillipillies, Harriet became so obsessed with the vision of sandy shores and rolling waves that it seemed altogether too inviting to be forgotten. Here was just the adventure she had been craving, and she was experienced enough to know that the opportunity might not come again. Next time, Dinny would perhaps not ask Harriet to be her companion—already the Barley Creek girl was more than a little scornful of the rules and regulations which surrounded her friend.

'And yet', thought Harriet, pausing to look up through the lillipillies' dripping leaves, which remained steadfast and unchanged throughout the autumn, 'I daren't ask Mother. She would certainly say "no". Father might let me go, if he were here—or Aidan might come with us. Oh, *bother* being a girl!'

She was silent and sullen during dinner, and immediately afterwards went to her room to fling herself face down on her bed. She was so still that Rose-Ann dared not address her, and was consequently taken by surprise when Harriet sat up, pushed back her hair, and said dramatically: 'I *shall* go, so there!'

Rose-Ann merely stared at her.

'You're supposed to ask me where I'm going,' Harriet said sharply.

'Why?' demanded Rose-Ann. 'You're always saying you're going to Africa, or China, or some other queer place. You haven't gone yet.'

'Don't be impertinent,' Harriet said, in an attempt to imitate her mother's voice. 'This time I *am* going, but not as far as China. I'm going to Winneroo.'

'Where's that?'

'It's a place at the seaside, five miles away. Dinny asked me to go with her, tomorrow. And you're to help me.'

'You don't want me to go too, do you?' asked Rose-Ann nervously.

'Of course not. You could never walk as far as that. Why, it will be ten miles, there and back. No, you must wait half an hour after I've gone, and then tell Mother. And be sure to tell her it's perfectly safe, that I'll be home before dark, and that I'm taking my dinner.'

'But, Harriet!' protested the horrified Rose-Ann. 'Whatever will Mother say? And Father, too, when he comes home.'

'I intend to be as good as good afterwards,' Harriet assured her. 'I shall practise all morning, and sew all afternoon. This will be my only adventure—I do think it's time I had one.'

'What if it rains?'

Harriet glared at her sister.

'It won't rain. I'll *make* it not rain.'

Rose-Ann was quite convinced next morning that Harriet was strong-minded enough to influence even the weather. For the day dawned fresh and clear and calm, with blue sky and benevolent sun. At a quarter to seven Harriet was fully dressed, and the early light transformed her sandy hair into a most unsuitable halo, as she addressed the drowsy Rose-Ann.

'Now don't forget to tell Mother everything—but not till half past seven. She doesn't usually come out till then, anyway.'

'All right,' mumbled Rose-Ann unhappily. 'I do think you're mad, Harriet.'

Unperturbed, Harriet crept around to the back door, and so into the kitchen, where Polly was already at work.

'Please, Polly, may I have some bread and cheese? Only don't ask what it's for.'

'Goin' off without your breakfast, are you?' said Polly. 'Never mind, I won't ask no questions. There's some bread cut on the table, an' you know where to find the butter and cheese.'

Harriet hastily made herself some rough but substantial sandwiches, to which the kind-hearted Polly added an apple and a lavish handful of raisins. Carefully Harriet wrapped her booty in a handkerchief of Aidan's and stowed it in her pocket.

'Good-bye, Polly—I'll see you at tea,' and before the surprised Polly could make any remark, Harriet was off, racing across the back yard. The path down the hill from the cowshed was familiar ground to her now, and she knew how to dodge the prickly vines and the bunches of sword-grass, even at top speed.

Dinny was waiting at the fence, barefooted and bare-headed as usual, for the mild May weather did not qualify as the season for donning boots or caps—June would be time enough for that.

'I didn't think you'd come,' she remarked, in pleased astonishment. 'I was just going to wait a bit, in case, but I never thought your Ma would say "yes".'

'Well, as a matter of fact, she didn't,' confessed Harriet. 'Do you mind if I eat my apple now, Dinny? I haven't had any breakfast.'

'Ma will give you some,' said Dinny. 'It won't matter if we're a bit late starting.'

'Oh, no,' said Harriet hurriedly. 'Let's start now. Which way do we go?'

Dinny put her hand in Harriet's—a rare gesture, for Dinny was the most undemonstrative of mortals.

'Come on, then. An' don't you worry about what they'll say—just tell 'em it was all my fault.'

Harriet smiled gratefully, and they set off along the Deacon's Flat road.

'We turn off here half a mile along,' explained Dinny. 'After that it's mostly up an' down all the way, over the hills.'

'Do we go near the swamp?' asked Harriet eagerly.

'You mean Heron Swamp? We don't have to cross it, thank goodness, but you can see part of it from the track. What do you know about the swamp, anyway?'

Harriet told her of Aidan's journey, and Dinny was suitably impressed.

'He must of been real brave to go down there at night. That's where the bunyip lives. An' that swamp hasn't got no bottom in places, Pa says.'

Once they left the road, Harriet's initial uneasiness began to wear off, for everything conspired to make her feel cheerful —the gentle sunlight, the mirth of nearby kookaburras, the company of Dinny. The track curved gradually along a hill-side, where moss shone bright green beneath the trees, and faint rustlings told of bandicoots and possums seeking their day-time refuge. Below, blue smoke rose straight up into the clear air from the houses of Barley Creek: far to the right, beyond the forest of bluegums, one isolated plume showed the whereabouts of Lillipilly Hill. Harriet was quite thankful when they turned to the left again, and all traces of habitation were left behind.

'We should be at Winneroo before nine,' said Dinny, her bare feet padding steadily along the stony track. 'Then we can stay on the beach for hours—we won't have to leave till about four.'

'Won't your father want to talk to you?' asked Harriet, resolutely putting to the back of her mind the thought of those eleven long hours away from home. She had expected to be at Lillipilly Hill in time for tea.

'Oh, he'll be busy,' said Dinny. 'He ain't much of a one for talking, anyway. Ma does all the talking for him. He likes me to keep out of the way when I go to Winneroo—I might get caught in the timber when they're loading. Once Joe sat down right in the middle of the tramway to eat his dinner, an' the truck nearly killed him. Pa never forgot that. He makes us go 'way down the beach now.'

It all sounded very strange and exciting to Harriet, and in her eagerness to see Winneroo for herself, she kept up valiantly with Dinny, although she had never before been obliged to walk so fast. Dinny seemed absolutely tireless as she marched along beneath the spiky branches of a line of she-oaks, which twisted downhill into yet another gully.

'When we get to the top of the next hill, we'll see the swamp, an' the sea an' everything,' she promised. 'Keep to the track—there's bound to be leeches after all the rain.'

'Leeches?' repeated Harriet, peering in horror at the scrub on either side. 'What do they look like?'

'Oh, you'd hardly notice 'em at first,' said Dinny cheerfully. 'They're sort of like black threads. But when they're on you, they get fatter an' fatter, an' you can't get 'em off, not without salt.'

If Harriet had been walking fast already, she now positively ran. She was well ahead of Dinny as they scrambled up the rocky slope out of the gully, and not until they were right at the top did she stop to regain her breath.

'Would you please look and see if there are any leeches on me?' she asked imploringly, and with unusual patience Dinny examined her companion's stockings and the hem of her dress.

'Can't find any,' came the reassuring verdict. 'They wouldn't of hurt you, anyhow.'

At last Harriet turned to look at the view, and the leeches were forgotten. Aidan's swamp, just as immense and lonely as he had described it, stretched away to the right, a vast pattern of glittering water and dark green reed-beds. Ahead, the land fell in a series of low, sparsely-covered ridges to the golden shore and the blue, beckoning sea.

'Winneroo's over there,' said Dinny, pointing to a steep headland on the left. 'The timber-yard is the other side of that hill. There's only about another mile to go.'

It was an enchanted mile to Harriet. The track broadened and flattened, and the soil was soft and sandy, yellowish-grey in colour, and pleasant underfoot. The tall gums and turpentines gave way to lower, more sprawling trees—creamy paperbarks, whose spongy trunks Harriet delighted to poke, and slender-leaved bottlebrushes, some bearing wiry, scarlet flowers. Harriet picked one or two, but immediately dropped them when she found that they were alive with tiny black ants.

Across the ridges drifted the sound of waves, and as they drew nearer to the headland, with it came a medley of other noises—clankings, hissings, and metallic rumblings. Filled with excitement, Harriet began to run, until she reached the top of the hill and felt the wonderful salt sea-breeze on her face and in her hair. At first she gazed in delight at the long yellow beach, with its pure clean sand, and its shining edges where seagulls walked beside the waves. Presently, however, she became aware that the slope below her was a hive of activity, to which the noises she had heard were directly related.

'My Pa must be down there somewhere,' said Dinny, indicating the group of men engaged in piling shingles on to a truck. 'When the truck's full, it runs down those lines to the wharf. The mill's just up there in the trees—that noise is the engine that drives the saws. Joe told me all about it once.'

Harriet could see now that the headland curved in a protective fashion around a little bay, a calm, sheltered place ideal for the mooring of boats. At the end of the wharf, rocking very gently on the breast of the pale-green water, were two ketches, one fully loaded and ready to sail.

'That's the *Winneroo Star*,' said Dinny. 'She's one of the old ones. They don't use the ketches much now—they've got real steamers, to carry the big timber. Pa went on one last summer, all the way to Sydney. I've never been to Sydney—Joe says he'll take me one day.'

They began to pick their way down the slope, keeping well clear of the tramway. Several of the men called a greeting to Dinny, and stared curiously at Harriet.

'Who's the carrot-top?' asked one youth, a weedy, thin-faced creature whom Harriet instinctively disliked.

'No business of yours, Alf Turner,' returned Dinny, taking Harriet's arm to hurry her past the group.

'He's the meanest of the lot,' Dinny whispered. 'No one likes him. They say old Bentley's just dying to get rid of him. But he ain't done nothing really bad—not yet. There's Pa, waving to us.'

Pinky O'Brien was a tough, stocky, squarely-built man, with the thick black hair his children had inherited, and skin the colour of mahogany from constant exposure to the sun. He had spent most of his life in the timber trade, beginning among the cedar forests of the North Coast, and no power on earth would have lured him to an indoor existence, or a job that confined him to one place. After a few days with his family, he grew restless, and could hardly wait to be back in the bush, or on the salty Winneroo hill-side.

He grunted rather than spoke to Dinny, nodded off-handedly to Harriet, and began to investigate the contents of the sack his daughter gave him. The splitter's rations were adequate, but hardly luxurious, consisting mainly of black tea, damper, and salt beef. Therefore the few extra delicacies sent out to him now and then by his wife were greeted with as much enthusiasm as Pinky could ever express.

'Joe's out sawing,' he told Dinny, meanwhile stuffing tobacco into his ancient black pipe. 'You won't see 'im this trip. Tell your Ma I'll be 'ome at the end of the month. You staying all day?'

'My word,' said Dinny. 'Harriet here ain't seen a beach like this one, have you, Harriet? Come on—let's go on the sand.'

The sun had not yet warmed the beach, being still quite low over the horizon—the girls had made good time, and it was barely nine o'clock. The sand was cool and damp, and at every step Harriet's boots left a print so perfect that she kept stopping to admire it.

'Why don't you go barefoot?' demanded Dinny. 'Then we can paddle.'

After all, thought Harriet, this was a day of rebellion, so why not be thorough? She sat down

169

and stripped off the heavy boots and stockings, and wriggled her toes ecstatically.

'That feels good,' she sighed. 'I wish I could go like this always. I'll leave my boots here, then we can get them afterwards. Let's run!'

They raced to the edge of the waves, and let the creamy water surge about their ankles, gasping a little at the first shock of cold. Then they laughed and jumped, running as far out as they dared, and leaping back just in time as the next wave curved and fell before them. Harriet had never been so happy. Sky and sea and beach seemed to stretch on for ever, and Lillipilly Hill belonged to another world.

'Come on—let's go round to the rocks,' suggested Dinny. 'We'd better go there now, before the tide's too high.'

The shelf below the headland was an intricate pattern of pools and crevices and tiny caves, each filled with tinted stones and miniature forests of weeds, spotted, striped, and fluted shells, and fish so small and fragile that Harriet had to lie flat on the rock to see them. In the larger crevices, crabs scuttled about with faint rattling sounds—some had bodies as big as saucers, and legs to match.

'If I had a spear, I could catch some for dinner,' boasted Dinny. 'Pa brings lots of 'em home with him.

An' fish, too, sometimes—an' once he caught an eel bigger'n Pete.'

'Don't talk about home now,' said Harriet dreamily. 'I don't want to think about going back.'

They sat on the rock with their backs to the land, and watched the *Winneroo Star* put out to sea, dipping gracefully and easily past the point, despite her full load.

'She's much prettier than a steam packet,' said Harriet. 'I would like to sail on her, a long way, until we came to a desert island with a blue lagoon, and lots of palms, and coloured birds.'

'She's only going to Sydney,' said Dinny practically. 'And that'd be far enough for me. When I grow up, I'm going to Sydney to live. I'll get some work there, and ride on the omnibuses, and go to the theatre—Ma told me all about it.'

'What sort of work will you do?' asked Harriet curiously. She tried hard to imagine a grown-up Dinny, with boots and piled-up hair, and even a hat. It was a real test of her imagination.

'I dunno,' said Dinny indifferently. 'I s'pose I'll have to work in someone's house, one of those big houses, like the Bentleys', in Blackhill—an upstairs an' a downstairs, and a little square thing on top, with all

171

that fancy iron stuff on it. Only Ma says the Sydney houses are even grander than that.'

'Being grown-up seems such a bother,' lamented Harriet. 'Then I shall have to look tidy every minute of the day, and never ever run or shout, or play hide-and-seek. I think I shall hate it.'

'Oh, no, you won't,' said Dinny positively. 'You'll have lovely clothes, an' little straw hats with flowers on, an' you won't never have to do anything but sit an' wait for some rich man to come an' marry you. I think you're lucky.'

But Harriet could only shudder at this dismal picture of her future, and change the subject.

'Is it time for dinner yet? I'm hungry.'

'Dunno what the time is, but the men haven't knocked off for their dinner. So it's not midday. Let's go round the point a bit—the tide doesn't come up this far.'

On the other side of the headland they found a narrow inlet, with a strip of unmarked, deep golden sand, and barriers of rock that shut out all sound except the murmur of the sea.

'Has this place got a name?' asked Harriet, gazing round in delight.

'Not that I know of,' answered Dinny. 'It's too small to be of any use to the mill.'

'I'm going to call it Harriet Bay, then. I've always wanted to have a place named after me,' said Harriet. 'It makes me feel like a real explorer. I shall tell Aidan about it as soon as he comes back.'

'If I called a place after meself, it would be somewhere a lot grander than this,' said Dinny contemptuously. 'I'd choose one big enough to be on Mr Burnie's globe, an' all the boys an' girls at school would have to learn it.'

But Harriet surveyed her territory with proprietary pride, and set about writing its name with shells in the sand, above the high-tide mark. When this was done, Dinny, who had been watching with an air of amused indulgence, glanced at the position of the sun and declared that it must be dinner-time.

'I wish I'd asked Polly for twice as much,' sighed Harriet, searching for the last crumbs. 'I've never been so hungry in my life.'

To take her mind off the subject of food, and the uneasy thought that many hours must pass before she would eat again, Harriet suggested building a sand-castle.

'What's that?' demanded Dinny, whose busy life held little opportunity for play.

So Harriet showed her, and presently Dinny began to build a castle of her own, becoming so absorbed that she ignored the passing of time, and let the tide creep up almost to her toes, and then recede again, without noticing. It was Harriet who finally abandoned her elaborate, shell-encrusted towers and looked up to see the sun's rays slanting over the headland.

'It must be getting late, Dinny. Should we be going?'

At once Dinny ceased to be a child at play, and became her usual self—an overworked girl with a number of responsibilities. She sprang up.

'Gracious, yes—it must be at least four o'clock. We'll go up the cliff—it's quicker.'

Each gave a backward glance as they began to climb—Dinny at her sand-castle, and Harriet at the brave row of shells, claiming the tiny bay as her own. Scrambling over the prickly grass and the sharp rocks of the cliff, she wondered if she would ever come here again, or whether her territory would be left to the seagulls and the waves.

Dinny did not wait to say good-bye to her father, who had gone back to the mill, but set off immediately towards the track, at a pace which Harriet found rather trying. In the shady hollow beyond the headland, Harriet suddenly stopped and wailed.

'Dinny! My boots!'

Dinny groaned.

'You *are* stupid! Oh, well, we'll just have to go

back for them—you'd never walk five miles without them.'

But Harriet's forgetfulness for once proved to be fortunate. As she and Dinny returned from the beach with the recovered footwear, a horse and buggy appeared on the road coming down from the mill. It was a very smart turn-out, the buggy shining with newness and plenty of polish, and the young chestnut horse fairly bursting with energy and spirit. The driver was a well-dressed, elderly man with thick, white hair and a trim, pointed beard.

'It's old Bentley,' said Dinny, stepping to the side of the road. 'That's the buggy he uses to drive himself around. When he's at home in Blackhill, he has the biggest carriage you've ever seen.'

To their surprise, Mr Bentley reined in his horse just as he was passing the girls, and peered intently at Dinny.

'You're an O'Brien, aren't you? I can take you part of the way home, if that's where you're going.'

Dinny needed no further invitation. She climbed nimbly up on to the seat, followed more diffidently by Harriet.

'Who is the other little girl?' asked Mr Bentley, as they set off at a brisk trot along the ridge. 'I haven't seen her out here before.'

Matthew Bentley, although nearly seventy, knew not only each of his many employees, but their wives and children as well. When money was scarce, or illness came, gifts were apt to arrive anonymously in a mill-worker's cottage, and everyone knew who was responsible. Not one of the workers' wives would have spoken a harsh word about Mr Bentley.

Encouraged by the old man's friendliness, Harriet explained who she was, and where she lived. Mr Bentley looked at her with keen interest.

'It you're one of the Wilmots, then what are you doing journeying round the countryside like this? Don't you have a governess?'

'We did, but she left,' said Harriet. 'And now we go to the Barley Creek school, and Father thinks we shall stay at Lillipilly Hill, instead of going back to London. He wasn't sure, at first.'

'Bit of a change for you all, I dare say,' remarked Mr Bentley. 'But it would have been even more of a change if you had come here forty-five years ago, as I did. Winneroo was just a camping-place for the blacks, and there wasn't a house between here and Blackhill. I started up my mill with a gang of convicts, and my own bare hands. All the timber was carried by bullock-dray to Blackhill Point, and then shipped. The mail came by horseback to Pittwater, and then by boat across to Blackhill Bay. And now there's to be a railway through Blackhill before the end of the year.'

'Then all your timber will go by rail, won't it?' asked Harriet, who was deeply interested in all these details.

'Well, yes, I suppose so, but you know, now that everything is made easy for us, we don't have the trade we used to have. People don't need shingles when they can get sheet iron—it's much better for roofing, you see, because the new shingles can taint the water that runs off them into the tanks. Once we used to supply a lot of cedar for floors and furniture, but that's all gone now. I believe that in another ten years Bentley's might have to close down, or else start all over again as another business.'

'But what will my Pa do then?' demanded Dinny, pouncing on the one feature of the story that had any interest for her.

'Oh, there will be work enough for everyone, I'm sure,' said Mr Bentley. 'Blackhill will be an important town with the railway coming, and one day this is going to be a great farming district—you mark my words. And tell your father, young lady,' he added, turning to Harriet, 'if he wants any help in planning his farm, to come to me. That hill would support a magnificent orchard.'

Harriet nodded eagerly, thinking that her encounter with Mr Bentley had indeed been doubly fortunate. She leant back luxuriously against the well-padded seat, and gazed up at the treetops as they seemed to flash across the fading sky. The track she and Dinny had followed that morning would have been impossible for any vehicle—instead, they took a less direct route that eventually brought them on to the Deacon's Flat road about a mile from Dinny's house.

'I'm afraid you'll have to get down here,' said Mr Bentley. 'I'm going on to Deacon's Flat to spend the night with my son. Good luck to you, and don't forget to tell your father about my offer, Miss Harriet.'

The steady clip-clop of the horse's hooves died away into the quiet distance, and Dinny and Harriet began to run.

'I do hope you don't catch it too hard,' panted Dinny. 'I s'pose I shouldn't have asked you to come, but I'm glad you did.'

'So am I,' said Harriet fervently. 'I wouldn't have missed it for anything. I shall see you again when school starts.'

They parted outside the O'Briens' shack, and Harriet scrambled up the hill, suddenly conscious of her torn pinafore, her sandy boots, and a lost hairribbon. Once within the boundary of home, she began to realize the enormity of what she had done. The sun was already dipping out of sight behind the bluegums as she crossed the silent yard and crept into the kitchen.

Turning from the stove, Polly, gave a startled jump, and almost dropped the huge, steaming kettle.

'Mercy, you gave me a fright! What a day you've given us—your poor mother *has* been in a state!'

'Have you had tea?' asked Harriet, not very hopefully.

''Course we have—hours ago. I'm just gettin' your sister's bath. You'd better go and see your mother. It's as well for you your father ain't home.'

Mrs Wilmot was in the sitting-room, doing nothing, apparently, except waiting for Harriet. And Harriet could only hang her guilty head and let the storm break—though in a secret part of her mind the vision of blue and gold shores still shone bright and clear.

10

Harriet's Bushranger

It was her father who finally made Harriet understand the seriousness of her escapade. He returned home on the following Monday to find Harriet confined to the house in deepest disgrace, awaiting his verdict. Harriet was by this time feeling rather sorry for herself, having decided that her mother was making a somewhat unnecessary fuss about the whole thing.

'You see, Harriet,' explained Mr Wilmot, 'you've almost spoilt all our plans—and they were *your* plans, you remember.'

'What do you mean?' asked Harriet, forgetting the attitude of noble and dignified suffering that she had decided to adopt.

'You wanted us all to stay here, and to make this our home. And to do that, you had to prove to your mother that you could still grow up in the way she wanted—in fact, that you would not turn into a little savage, through living in the bush. I believe you promised to do just as she asked.'

Harriet thought back to the March day when her father had told her of his decision to stay on at Lillipilly Hill. It seemed quite remote now—she had taken it for granted in the past weeks that they would always remain here.

'I think I did,' she muttered.

'I'm sure you did. You expected Aidan to help you with your plans, and he very obligingly did so. Rose-Ann has done her best, too, although she has had to give up a great many things that she likes, by staying here. But what have *you* done, Harriet, to show us that you deserve to have your way?'

'I did try,' protested Harriet. 'I practised my music, and I sewed ever so many seams, and I've learnt to do my own hair. I've never run away before—it was because I had nothing to do, and Dinny wanted me to go with her. I know Mother doesn't like Dinny—'

'Your mother has no objection to Dinny at all,' said Mr Wilmot firmly. 'From what we hear, she's an extremely hard-working child, and the family is perfectly respectable. But that does not alter the fact that you deceived your mother, and worried her to such an extent that she is now seriously considering returning to London, taking you and Rose-Ann with her.'

Harriet stared at him in horrified surprise.

'She won't really, will she? Is it just because of me?'

'Mostly because of you, yes,' answered Mr Wilmot. 'She is afraid that either you will do yourself some physical harm if you wander off again, or that you will turn into a creature little better than a gipsy. So you see, Harriet, you've almost ruined your own plan—and I think it was quite a good one. I should much prefer all of us to stay here together.'

'I won't run away again, I promise—I won't even leave the garden, except to go to school. Truly I won't!' cried Harriet despairingly. 'Please tell Mother that, and ask her not to take us back to London!'

'You must tell her yourself. We agreed in the beginning to have six months' trial here—that arrangement will stand. But if at the end of that time we are not satisfied with this as a way of life for you girls, then your mother and you and Rose-Ann will leave immediately.'

Harriet made a rapid calculation. This was the middle of May—so she had until the end of September to redeem herself. Her usual optimism came to the surface again.

'I'll be so good, Father, you won't know it's me. And I *have* been doing well at school—Mr Burnie said so.'

'I'm afraid, Harriet, that you will have no opportunity to be anything other than good in the next few weeks. We have decided that you will remain at home for a month, and that you will not go beyond the boundary fence during that time—except to church.'

'But what about school?' asked Harriet incredulously.

'You will not go to school. Mr Burnie will send up your lesson books, and you can study them at home. There will be plenty for you to do, helping your mother and Polly, and keeping up your music, until you begin your lessons again. When we are certain that you are to be trusted, you will return to school.'

Harriet reflected gloomily that she had every reason to be really sorry for herself now. The vision of the long, lonely, empty weeks ahead was almost too dreary to be borne. She turned towards the window, wondering if it would help to imagine herself a captured princess locked in a dungeon.

'Will I just get bread and water?' she asked, and for the first time that morning her father permitted himself to smile.

'I think perhaps Polly will feed you on something better than that,' he said. 'And if it's any consolation, I will help you with your lessons.'

'Oh, I nearly forgot!' Harriet exclaimed. 'I met Mr Bentley, the man who owns the timber-mill, and he told me to tell you that he knows all about orchards, if you wanted any help. You are going to plant an orchard, aren't you. Father?'

'I hope so. Where can I find this Mr Bentley?'

'I think he lives in Blackhill, when he's not at the mill. Dinny will know. I could go and ask—'

She broke off, remembering the terms of her imprisonment, and sighed.

'Oh, well, Rose-Ann could ask her. Will Dinny be allowed to come and see me?'

'I think not, at least for a week or two. Please remember, Harriet, that you are in disgrace.'

And so it happened, one June evening three weeks later, that Polly and Harriet were alone in the house. Mr and Mrs Wilmot had taken Aidan and Rose-Ann to Blackhill to hear a concert presented by members of the grandly-named Blackhill Dramatic and Musical Society. It was the social event of the year in the Blackhill district, and Rose-Ann had departed in a great state of excitement, wearing her new winter dress and a jaunty sailor hat. Polly had been warned that the family might stay the night at the Blackhill Hotel, rather than attempt the dark and cold ride home.

'They won't be back till morning, that's certain,' remarked Polly, as she and Harriet ate their tea in the kitchen. 'Listen to the rain!'

Harriet listened, and felt strangely content. At first her exclusion from the Blackhill visit had reduced her to a state of gloom and resentment, and she had been imagining the pleasures which Aidan and Rose-Ann must be experiencing while she sat miserably at home. But in Polly's company she could not remain low-spirited for long, and it was something of a treat to be allowed to have her tea at the kitchen table, in front of the huge, glowing stove. The heavy rain drummed on the iron roof, and splashed on to the tanks, while inside it was very warm and snug and peaceful. Polly had made pancakes for tea, and Harriet had just finished her fifth.

'You must be the best cook in the whole world, Polly,' she said blissfully. 'I can't eat any more now, but could I have some more pancakes for supper?'

'You're to go to bed at eight, the missus said,' Polly reminded her. 'Maybe you could have your supper in bed, though. It'd be a shame to waste those pancakes.'

At six o'clock it was quite dark, and Polly set off on a tour of the house, closing shutters, drawing curtains, and locking all the doors. Although Boz was officially in charge, his shack was more than a hundred yards away, and Polly was taking no chances, with rumours of bushrangers still rife. Harriet brought out *At the Back of the North Wind*, which was her favourite reading matter when she was feeling particularly contented and comfortable. The evening stretched ahead of her, cosy and uneventful.

There was a sudden loud banging at the back door, and Boz's voice summoned Polly from her rounds.

'If it's tea you want, you'll have to wait till the kettle boils again,' grumbled Polly. 'Don't stand out there in the rain.'

'I'm not after tea,' said Boz. 'I'd rather drink me own brew, thank you. I want a hand—one of the cows is out, an' you'll have to help me get her in. Bring a lamp.'

'Drat the old cow! I'm not s'posed to leave Harriet here by herself.'

'She can't come to no harm. Lock her in—we won't be long, if you'll just get a move on.'

Complaining volubly, Polly donned a man's old felt hat, took off her apron, and prepared to follow Boz.

'And mind you just stay where you are,' she told Harriet. 'Don't let the fire go out, neither.'

It was very quiet when they had gone. The rain had eased to a monotonous drizzle, hardly audible, although there were still a number of little splashing sounds from the verandas, where the gutters had overflowed. These made a pleasant background to Diamond's adventures, and Harriet lifted her head from time to time, reflecting that the splashing noises were very like a whispering voice. Presently she let the book fall to her lap, for the voice was actually speaking.

'Let me in!' it said. 'Let me in!'

Harriet sprang up. Undoubtedly it was a real voice, and quite a loud one, for it soon gave up any pretence of whispering. It came from the back door, and it belonged to neither Polly nor Boz.

'A bushranger!' thought Harriet immediately, and she tried desperately to make some sort of plan, in case the intruder forced the door or a window. It was no use calling for Boz—he would be away beyond the cow-paddock, out of earshot. And as far as Harriet knew, there were no weapons of any kind in the house, even had she been prepared to use them. The only thing to do seemed to be far too simple and irksome for Harriet—namely, just to sit and wait until Boz and Polly returned, as they must surely do before very long. Instead, she summoned all her courage, and went towards the door.

'Who's there?' she demanded in her most grown-up voice, which none the less was a trifle wobbly.

'I ain't saying,' was the definite answer.

'What do you want?'

The reply was quite unexpected.

'I want to see Aidan,' said the voice.

By this time Harriet had reached one certain conclusion—the intruder, bushranger or not, was quite young. And he sounded more upset than ferocious. So Harriet opened the door.

At first she thought she had made a terrible mistake. The grimy, bedraggled appearance of Clay did little to reassure her, and in the dark of the yard his suntanned face and black eyes were more than a little alarming. Harriet drew back, intending to slam the door, but Clay was too quick for her.

'I want to see Aidan,' he repeated, stepping into the kitchen, and closing the door behind him.

'Aidan's not here,' said Harriet. She retreated towards the table, wondering whether the poker was in its usual place near the stove. She might be able to reach it behind her back—

'Where is he, then?' demanded Clay, scowling

beneath the brim of his battered old hat. 'Are you Harriet?'

'Yes, I am,' said Harriet in surprise. 'Aidan's gone in to Blackhill, and he won't be back till morning. Whatever do you want?'

Clay sat down dispiritedly in Harriet's chair. He no longer looked intimidating, and Harriet stopped trying to reach the poker. Her curiosity had by now got the better of her, anyway.

'Aidan didn't tell you about me, did he?' asked Clay.

Harriet shook her head, and Clay looked strangely pleased.

'Good—I didn't think he would. I'm Clay. Aidan knows me, an' he knows my dog—that's what I've come about. Patchy got her leg caught in a trap, an' I can't look after her right. I reckoned Aidan'd help me.'

'Patchy is the dog?' asked Harriet, sitting down opposite Clay. 'By the way, would you like some pancakes? Polly makes wonderful pancakes, and there are plenty left.'

Clay nodded hungrily, and Harriet produced the remains of her tea. Clay did not speak again until every crumb had been eaten.

'I should of fed Patchy first,' he said guiltily. 'But I ain't had nothing since breakfast, an' anyway, I left Patchy down by the shed.'

'Couldn't I help with Patchy?' asked Harriet eagerly. 'I like dogs, and it's awful to think of her out in the rain. Why don't you bring her in here?'

Clay looked doubtfully round the orderly, well-scrubbed kitchen.

'What'd your Polly say?'

'She won't mind,' said Harriet, with more confidence than she really felt. 'I'll warm up some milk, shall I? Does Patchy drink milk?'

'She never gets nothing but water when she's at home,' said Clay.

'Where's home?' asked Harriet. 'I haven't seen you in Barley Creek before.'

Clay looked at her suspiciously.

'You're a lot nosier than your brother. *He* never asked too many questions.'

'Haven't I got a right to ask questions?' demanded Harriet indignantly. 'You come banging at our door in the dark, and stamping into our kitchen, and eating our pancakes, and then you won't even tell me where you live. For all I know, you could be a bushranger, just as I thought at first.'

'Me name's Clay, an' I ain't a bushranger, though there's people ready to say I am. That's all I'll tell you. Now can I bring Patchy in, or can't I?'

'All right,' said Harriet. 'But "Clay" is the queerest name I ever heard.'

She poured a lavish quantity of milk into one of Polly's best saucepans, and set it on the stove. The rain had become heavy again, and when Clay returned, both he and the animal he was laboriously carrying were thoroughly wet. Harriet tried to pat the dog's head, but Patchy at once bared her teeth and snarled.

'She won't let anyone but me touch her,' Clay warned her. 'She ain't used to people. If she wasn't sick, she'd never of come in.'

He put Patchy on the floor near the stove, and sat down beside her. With his hat off, and his head bent over his dog in anxious affection, he seemed much younger and more vulnerable. Harriet knelt on the hearth and peered as closely as she dared at the injured leg. It hung limp and useless, and when Clay touched it, Patchy whimpered in pain. It was thus that the startled Polly found the three of them as she burst into the kitchen.

'Whatever is this? What mischief are you up to now, Harriet? Strike me pink, but you're a handful.'

'It's not mischief at all,' protested Harriet. 'This is Clay—he's a friend of Aidan's, and he's come here because his dog got hurt in a trap.'

Polly stared grimly at Clay, who kept his head down and did not speak.

'Friend of Aidan's, is he? Does your father know about him? Not likely! Looks more like a tramp, if you ask *me*. I'm going to get Boz.'

'Please, Polly!' begged Harriet. 'Don't tell Boz. I'll explain to Father in the morning. Clay hasn't done anything wrong, and I'm sure Patchy's leg is broken. Look—come and see.'

'I don't like dogs,' said Polly, but none the less she let Harriet drag her across to the stove and point out the extent of Patchy's injury.

'That needs putting in a splint—I've seen 'em doing it to my young brother when he fell out of a tree an' broke his arm. You get two pieces of board, see, an' fix 'em round the leg with a bit of rag.'

Two eager faces gazed up at her, and Harriet spoke for them both.

'Won't you do it to Patchy, Polly? I'll find some boards and some rag. You will, won't you? I know Father would do it if he were here. He likes animals.'

With a show of reluctance, Polly gave in.

'An' what's that milk doing boiling all over my clean stove? Just take it off, Harriet, an' if it's for that mongrel dog, then put it in an old tin plate. It'd be just like you to use the best dinner plates.'

Harriet meekly obeyed, then went off to search for the boards. When she returned, Polly was making a pot of tea, and setting out three cups, while Patchy lapped feebly at the milk.

'If you let that there dog bite me, you'll be out of here in the wink of an eye,' Polly said to Clay. 'Just hold her still.'

There were few things Polly could not set her hand to if she chose, and her manipulation of Patchy's leg was amazingly sure and quick. Patchy seemed to realize that someone trustworthy was in charge, and lay quite still in Clay's grasp. In a very short time Polly was standing back admiring her handiwork.

'Neat, ain't it? But it'll come off if she moves around. How far do you have to take her?'

'A good way,' muttered Clay. ''Bout four mile.'

'But you can't walk as far as that in all the rain, not carrying Patchy,' objected Harriet. 'Can't they stay here, Polly?'

'Not in the house, they can't,' said Polly firmly. 'I'd never dare tell the missus I'd let a stranger sleep here, not knowing nothing about him. But he's welcome to that new pile of chaff bags in the cowshed.'

'That'll do,' said Clay. 'I wouldn't stay here at all, if it wasn't for Patchy. An' I'll be gone soon as it's light.'

'If you've got any sense, you'll leave that dog here for a while,' declared Polly. 'If you go moving her around, that leg mightn't set right. If she stays still for a few days, it'll be as good as new in next to no time.'

'She'd fret without me,' protested Clay. 'She ain't never been away from me before.'

Polly shrugged.

'Do as you please, then. Here's your tea—help yourself to sugar. An' drink yours up quick, Harriet—it's time you were in bed.'

But Harriet managed to make her tea last until Clay gathered up his burden and set off for the cowshed.

'If you do leave Patchy, we'll all look after her,' she promised. 'She'll have plenty to eat, and we'll take it in turns to stay with her.'

'I dunno,' said Clay. 'I s'pose she ought to stay.'

'Couldn't you stay, too?' asked Harriet. 'Father would let you sleep in the cowshed.'

But Clay shook his head.

'No—there'd be too many questions. I could come back an' see her though, couldn't I? After dark, so as people wouldn't notice me.'

'Why does it matter if people see you?' demanded Harriet. 'You're just a boy with a dog.'

'There you go, asking questions again,' grumbled Clay. 'I'm off. I'll sleep in your shed tonight, but I'll be gone first thing in the morning.'

He and Patchy disappeared into the darkness, and Polly exclaimed, 'How d'you like that! Not even a "thank you". I reckon he ain't been taught any manners.'

'I'd love to know who he is, and where he lives, and everything,' said Harriet wistfully. 'I wonder if Aidan will tell me.'

She was determined to see Clay in the morning, but although she tiptoed out to the cowshed at dawn, it was already empty—save for a frantic Patchy chained to a post. She snarled at Harriet, refused a proffered gift of a crust of bread, and continued to tug at her chain, her mournful eyes focussed on the orchard slip-rail through which Clay must have gone.

'Patchy, you're supposed to be resting,' said Harriet anxiously. 'Clay will come back tonight, I'm sure he will.'

But Patchy's only answer was a long-drawn howl, which brought Boz in from the paddock.

'Where on earth did this mongrel come from?' he asked, keeping at a safe distance from Patchy's snapping jaws.

Harriet explained, and Boz gave a scornful grunt.

'That Polly's gone daft, letting strangers and savage dogs into the house at night. I've heard of a boy that roams round hunting rabbits near Maloney's Hill—always has a blue cattle-dog with him. Could be the thief everyone's talking about.'

'Clay isn't a thief,' said Harriet indignantly. 'He's one of Aidan's friends. You wait until Aidan comes back—he'll tell you.'

But when Aidan arrived home with the rest of the family in the middle of the morning, after a damp and muddy drive, he had very little information to offer. It took him some five minutes to unravel Harriet's excited and incoherent story, and then he went immediately to the cowshed to see Patchy.

'That's Clay's dog, all right,' he said, trying unsuccessfully to pat the animal's head. 'And I don't wonder she's miserable—she goes everywhere with Clay. He'll be miserable, too.'

'Who is he? Where does he live? Has he got another name? Do tell me, Aidan—he's like someone out of a story.'

'I don't know anything about him, except where he lives, and I promised not to tell anyone that. Does Father know about Patchy?'

'I was going to tell him as soon as I'd seen you,' said Harriet. 'I do think you're mean, Aidan. Clay might be the missing heir to a fortune—a prince, even—and you could help to return him to his real home. It could be just like a story.'

'If you want a story, you'll have to make it up yourself,' declared Aidan, thereby giving his sister a pleasant and absorbing occupation for the rest of her imprisonment. Harriet wandered off to the front garden to think out the details of her plot, while Aidan sought out his father, and explained away the presence of a strange and most unfriendly dog chained up in the cowshed.

'I think we should know more about this Clay,' said Mr Wilmot. 'This is a wild country, with unfamiliar ways, but even so I don't believe that it's customary for boys to live alone in the bush. Tell him that we shall keep his dog until it's quite recovered, but that we should prefer him to come to the house openly whenever he calls.'

However, Aidan did not encounter Clay at all in the days that followed. Clay apparently made his visits at night, and not even Boz could discover his comings and goings. Once, after the rain had gone, and a full moon rode proudly across the sky, Aidan thought he caught a glimpse of a figure running from the cowshed towards the orchard, but by the time he had reached the back yard, the figure had vanished. So Mr Wilmot had to leave the mystery of Clay unsolved, and Harriet was free to invent her own highly romantic explanation.

There remained the problem of Patchy. For the entire day after her abandonment in the shed, she refused to eat or drink, no matter what delicacies were laid before her. She tried to bite Polly, she jumped at Boz's throat, and when left alone she howled incessantly. By sunset, the entire Wilmot household was in despair, and no one expected to sleep.

'There's only one of us who hasn't tried to make friends with her,' said Harriet at last. 'Where's Rose-Ann?'

'She'll be too frightened even to look at her,' said Aidan. 'Mother told her not to go near Patchy, in case Patchy bit her.'

But Rose-Ann, it appeared, was extremely anxious to make Patchy's acquaintance, and eventually she managed to persuade her mother to let her visit the shed. By now it was almost dark, and Patchy looked quite a fearsome sight, with bared teeth and glittering eyes.

'Don't go too close, Rose-Ann,' begged Aidan. 'Just put down the milk and come away.'

'But I like dogs,' protested Rose-Ann. 'Just because I'm frightened of spiders and snakes and things, you think I'm frightened of everything.'

'This isn't an ordinary dog,' Harriet pointed out. 'She's a wild animal—like a lion or a tiger.'

Rose-Ann approached Patchy very quietly, and set down the dish of milk. Patchy drew back suspiciously, and the grey-blue hair on her neck bristled like the quills of a porcupine. Rose-Ann crouched beside the dish and talked softly to the dog as she sometimes talked to her dolls when she believed Harriet to be out of earshot. Patchy lay down, her gaze now fixed on the milk. Perhaps she was merely very thirsty, and suddenly decided to give in, or perhaps she really did prefer the presence of Rose-Ann to that of anyone else save Clay—whatever the reason, she began to drag herself forward on her stomach, and, while the onlookers held their breath, she lapped up the entire contents of the dish. 'She wants some more,' whispered Harriet. 'I'll go and get it.'

While Patchy had her second drink, Rose-Ann crept closer. Presently her hand was on the dog's neck, and Patchy made no movement of protest. Soon Rose-Ann was stroking the strong, rough back, and Patchy was lying quietly with her nose between her paws. When at last Rose-Ann was called indoors, Patchy was fast asleep.

Thereafter Rose-Ann, highly delighted, was appointed Patchy's nursemaid, friend, and comforter. And although the dog eventually allowed the others to approach her, no one but Rose-Ann was permitted within patting distance. When the leg was pronounced sufficiently well mended for Patchy to return to Clay, and a note was left in the cowshed to that effect, Rose-Ann cried herself to sleep. The next morning Patchy was gone, and Mr Wilmot had to buy a kitten from a family in Barley Creek in an attempt to assuage his younger daughter's grief.

11

The Swamp

On a windy, boisterous, blustery morning late in June, Harriet went back to school. She felt like a traveller returned from a distant land as she took her place at the long desk, with Dinny beside her—still the old cheerful Dinny, despite her altered garb of worn serge and scuffed, over-large boots. A few changes had occurred in Harriet's absence—Paddy Tolly had been removed from school to help his mother in the shop, Aidan sat in the place of honour at the head of the back form, and one of the twins had broken an arm in a fall from the tallest pine tree. All these events Harriet discussed eagerly with Dinny and Rose-Ann and Maggie during the morning break, inside their old refuge—the disused tank.

'We all missed you,' Dinny assured the former exile. 'Rose-Ann told us what your Pa had done to you, an' we all thought it wasn't a bit fair.'

'My father never minds a bit if I go off anywhere on my own,' declared Maggie. 'He says I talk too much an' it makes him tired, after he's bin working in the dairy all day, with them cows mooing at him. He sends us all outside so he can have his tea in peace.'

'You ain't seen Harriet's place, though,' scoffed Dinny. 'They have a girl to do their cooking and washing an' all that, an' the house is so big you'd get lost in it ever so easy.'

'It's not nearly as big as our house in London,' said Rose-Ann, but Harriet interrupted her hurriedly.

'Don't boast, Rose-Ann—it doesn't matter one bit how big that house was, because we're never going back, anyway. And we only have Polly because Mother isn't strong enough to do all the work herself.'

'Oh, I know you ain't boasting,' said Dinny cheerfully. 'I'm going to have a much bigger house than yours one day, an' three or four maids all to myself.'

'I s'pose I'll just stay here an' work in the dairy,' said Maggie gloomily.

'We'll probably have to move somewhere else when the mill closes,' said Dinny. 'Pa might go to Blackhill an' work on the new railway. Did your father ever ask

Mr Bentley about how to plant orange trees, Harriet?'

'He's to see Mr Bentley tomorrow,' said Harriet. 'He wants to plant in the spring. Once the trees are planted, I just *know* we shan't go back to London. And Aidan is to sit for his scholarship in October. If he passes, he's to go to the Grammar School next year.'

But Maggie was bored by this talk of future plans, and brought the conversation back to the present.

'Did you hear about the bushranger? Only Pa says he's not really a bushranger, just an ordinary old thief. He took some money from Wilkins' dairy out at Deacon's Flat. John Wilkins chased him with a gun, but he got away. Had a dog with him, John said.'

'Lots of people have dogs,' murmured Harriet, suppressing a feeling of uneasiness. 'And Deacon's Flat is a long way from here.'

'Not all that far,' said Dinny. 'An' there's plenty of scrub to hide in. Well, if he comes looking for money in our place, he'll be out of luck. There's the bell—I'll race you, Harriet.'

The old routine of school, music lessons, sewing and practising was soon taken up again, and the short days of midwinter went rapidly by. Not that it ever seemed like winter here, Harriet thought— although in the early morning frost glittered on the roadside down on the flat, and evening mists wrapped themselves around the foot of Lillipilly Hill, the days were clear and fresh and golden, and the skies a milky blue. It was the sort of weather that made Harriet skip and run and long for adventure, but she managed to keep herself in check, remembering how much was at stake. She capered in a most unladylike way when she accidentally overheard her mother say to Mrs Farmer:

'I'm so pleased with the improvement in Harriet. It seems she is not turning into a little savage, after all.'

July came, and all seemed well at Lillipilly Hill. Mrs Wilmot appeared to be stronger and more cheerful than at any time since her arrival in New South Wales, Mr Wilmot watched Boz ploughing the orchard slope and planned his campaign for the coming months, Aidan spent happy, solitary hours with his books and his dreams, and Rose-Ann and her kitten grew plump and contented. Polly sang all day, indoors and out, and Steve Jackson, Barley Creek's cricket captain, was always to be seen waiting down on the track with his buggy, whenever Polly had her day off.

In the middle of July the weather changed abruptly. On a Friday morning Harriet woke to hear the shutters rattling and the vines rustling, and looked out to see the trees swooping downwards under a violent southerly gale. Grey rain swept across the garden, and blotted out the hills and valleys.

'I think you girls had better stay at home this morning,' said Mr Wilmot at breakfast. 'Aidan can go to school, and stay there for lunch. I'm afraid this weather has set in for the day.'

He was right. Instead of abating, the gale increased in strength, and Harriet spent the morning with her face at the kitchen window, watching the wild swinging and bending of branches, and the fierce onslaught of the rain, which turned the garden into a quagmire, and drenched the veranda floors. Once a limb from one of the blue-gums crashed on to the cowshed roof, and Barrel whinnied in fear.

'I should love to go out in it,' said Harriet. 'The wind's so strong it would lift me right off the top of the hill, and take me all the way to Winneroo. Wouldn't it be lovely to see the sea on a day like this, Rose-Ann?'

'No,' said Rose-Ann, who was sitting by the stove with her kitten. 'It would be like those awful storms when we were on the boat coming out. I'd much rather be here than outside.'

At dinner Polly reported that the creek had risen over the road at the ford, and Harriet was full of excitement.

'We'll be marooned up here, and we'll have to build a raft to go out for supplies. How much food have we got left, Polly?'

'Enough for a week at least,' said Polly witheringly. 'So you needn't go building no raft. This'll blow itself out by termorrow, you'll see.'

'And Aidan will be our scout, bringing back news of our position,' continued Harriet, unperturbed. 'He might have to swim the flooded river to get here.'

'If he has any sense, he'll come up the back way,' said Polly. 'He knows better than to get hisself half-drowned—not like some I could mention.'

Sure enough, Aidan arrived home by way of the western hill-side, and was at once bombarded with questions from Harriet as to the state of the township and the height of the creek.

'I don't know, I tell you,' he said crossly. 'I didn't wait to see what had happened. Do let me get my boots and coat off, Harriet—then I want to tell you something private.'

'My, we are getting swanky, when we can't talk in front of our elders and betters,' remarked Polly to the stove. 'An' don't put those muddy boots on my rug, Aidan.'

Eagerly and importantly, Harriet followed Aidan across the hall to his room. He shut the door, and marched over to the window; the grey light of the storm showed his face to be pale and worried, and Harriet's excitement gave way to anxiety.

'Whatever is it? Did something go wrong at school? Were the boys calling you names again?'

'Of course not,' said Aidan impatiently. 'I can look after myself, anyway. This is nothing to do with school, except that it was Bill Mackenzie who told me. It's about the thief—he broke into Tolly's store last night, and took most of the week's money.'

'Poor Mrs Tolly—what a shame! Did she see the thief?'

'She thinks she did. It was dark, and she couldn't be sure, but Paddy followed him for quite a long way, and he says it was a boy about his size, with a hat pulled down over his eyes. There was a dog, too—a blue cattle-dog.'

Harriet stared in horror at her brother.

'That sounds like Clay and Patchy, only it *couldn't* be. Paddy must have made a mistake—you know how stupid he is.'

'I think it was Clay he saw, certainly, but that doesn't mean Clay was the thief. He often traps rabbits in the evenings, and he would be carrying a bag, and trying not to be seen. He might look rather like a thief.'

'Only we know he isn't,' said Harriet quickly. 'We can tell Paddy he followed the wrong person.'

'D'you think Paddy would believe us?' asked Aidan scornfully. 'He's told all Barley Creek about it

now, and he says he knows where the thief lives, too—
out around Maloney's Hill. He must have followed
Clay a long way.'

'What will Paddy do, then? He's not going to try
to catch Clay, is he?'

'Not by himself,' said Aidan grimly. 'But a dozen
men from Barley Creek are going out first thing in the
morning—with guns.'

'You mean they'll be hunting for Clay? Just the
same as they would hunt a fox or rabbits?'

Aidan gazed out at the darkening garden, where
a miniature lake was being swept into rippling waves
by the wind.

'If they think Clay is the thief, you can't blame
them for trying to catch him, can you? The nearest
policeman is at Blackhill, and there's no way of
reaching him while the creek is up. They don't want
to waste time, either. Clay could be warned, and get
right away.'

'Who would warn him? He won't know anything
about it.'

'Yes, he will,' said Aidan. 'We're going to tell him,
Harriet. Clay isn't a thief—you know that, don't you?'

'Of course,' said Harriet. 'Thieves don't carry
their sick dogs for miles on a wet night. But how are
we to warn him?'

'Bill said the men are meeting at the store just as soon as it's light. That won't be until after six—it's awfully dark in the mornings now. If we left here at half past five, we'd be about an hour ahead of them, and if we ran most of the way, we should be able to give Clay a good start. He knows the country so well he'd soon find a hiding-place.'

'Are we going to tell Father?' asked Harriet.

She hardly knew her quiet, scholarly brother in the angry and determined youth who now confronted her.

'No—how can we? Father would *have* to stop us, because as far as he knows, Clay could be a thief or a bushranger or anything. But if you're afraid, you don't have to come. I can find Clay on my own.'

Harriet did some rapid and unhappy thinking. To her mother, this would be just another deplorable escapade, and to her father, the breaking of a promise. Both verdicts could mean nothing but the end of all her hopes, and a certain departure from Lillipilly Hill. But the picture in her mind was too vivid and terrifying— twelve men, with guns, advancing on an innocent and ignorant boy, believing himself secure on his lonely hill-top. Clearly, if she could help him in any way at all, she must do so.

'I'm not afraid,' she declared stoutly. 'And I promise I won't tell anyone. How are we going to find our way? We won't be able to see a thing at half past five.'

'We'll take my lamp,' said Aidan. 'And don't forget to wear your strongest boots, and a cap. It will be awfully wet. I'll wake you up at a quarter past five.'

'Tea's ready, you two!' called Polly from the kitchen, and the conspirators emerged into the familiar warmth and light of the dining-room.

'I wish you'd tell me your secret,' said Rose-Ann wistfully. 'I'm always being left out.'

'We'll tell you afterwards,' promised Aidan. 'It's not the sort of secret you'd like, anyway.'

Harriet gazed round the cosy, shabby little room, with its old, panelled walls, its hated piano, and its one shuttered window. Even the long weary hours of practice, and the endless seams stitched at this very table, seemed quite bearable now that they were viewed in retrospect, as part of a life that might soon be altered. Harriet tried to see herself as a noble heroine sacrificing everything in the course of duty, but it was no good—she only wanted to be plain Harriet Wilmot of Lillipilly Hill, not a languishing exile in a Kensington square. Her bread and butter suddenly tasted like sawdust, and she pushed away her plate.

'I'm going to bed,' she said. 'You can have my cake, Rose-Ann.'

She went into the sitting-room to say good night to her mother and father.

'It's only half past five, Harriet—is anything wrong?' asked Mrs Wilmot in surprise.

'No—I just want to go to bed,' said Harriet.

Mr Wilmot glanced up from some papers he had been studying.

'I must tell you, Harriet, as you're so interested in our plans for Lillipilly Hill, that we have just inherited a little extra money which will make it possible for us to plant at least five hundred trees this spring. Your mother says you will be allowed to help with the planting.'

Harriet summoned all her dignity to prevent herself from crying.

'If I'm not here in the spring, Father, then perhaps Aidan will plant my trees for me. I'd like an orange tree best.'

And, not trusting herself to say more, she left the room, while her parents exchanged glances of bewilderment.

'What extraordinary things that child says,' observed Mrs Wilmot. 'I think she reads too many stories. Why on earth shouldn't she be here in the spring?'

'Harriet,' said Mr Wilmot, 'has something on her mind. And whatever it is, it's quite weighty. Perhaps we shall find out tomorrow.'

Never had the darkness seemed as thick and impenetrable as on that July morning, when Aidan crept into the girls' room to rouse Harriet from a restless, dream-ridden sleep. He had left the lamp outside the door, so as not to disturb Rose-Ann, and Harriet had to grope for her clothes, shivering all the while. The wind had dropped during the night, and not the faintest sound invaded the silence of the house. It was bitterly cold, and Harriet was very grateful for the woollen muffler that Aidan thrust into her hand as she crept through the door. She wound it around her neck and pulled her cap well down over her ears.

'Go through the kitchen,' whispered Aidan. 'We'll take some bread as we go.'

The lamp threw eerie, dancing shadows across the kitchen wall, and Rose-Ann's kitten sprang away in alarm from her bed on the hearth. Harriet had no appetite for the hunk of dry bread which Aidan gave her, but she prudently tucked it into her pocket while Aidan slid back the heavy bolt of the back door. It creaked a little, and Harriet glanced fearfully towards the door of Polly's little room, beside the pantry.

However, Polly was making the most of her last hour of sleep, and did not stir.

The back yard was a black, squelching, sticky sea of mud. Harriet clung to the back of Aidan's jacket, and followed the feeble light of his lamp. At the top of the orchard, Aidan paused.

'This is the way I went before, and it's the only way I know. But if the creek's up as far as Polly says, it might be quite dangerous. Perhaps you ought to go back, after all.'

'No, I'm coming with you,' said Harriet firmly. 'I'm not going back across that yard by myself, anyway.'

They slithered and scrambled down the hill, past the ghostly, sodden trees and the glistening furrows left by Boz's plough. As they came closer to the creek, they could hear an ominous sound—the continuous gurgling and rushing of swollen water.

'I'm afraid Polly was right,' said Aidan. 'Look at that!'

He held his lamp high, and Harriet gazed in dismay at the creek, no longer the friendly and leisurely stream she knew, but a brown, angry, hasty torrent, which had engulfed its banks and the path beside it. The rocky slopes now fell sheer to the water's edge.

'What on earth shall we do now?' demanded Aidan. 'I'm sure I could never find a way round these hills in the dark.'

'If we can't get through, then those men won't either,' said Harriet hopefully.

'Of course they will. They've lived here all their lives, and they probably know a dozen different tracks. You'll have to go back, Harriet, and I'll go on by myself. It won't be so bad if just one of us gets lost.'

Suddenly, Harriet remembered a fine May morning, and Dinny's chatter.

'There *is* another way, Aidan! It's longer, but we could run part of it. We have to go along the Winneroo track, until we get to the swamp.'

'How do we cross the swamp?' asked Aidan, cautiously, but with the beginnings of a new hope.

'Oh, I don't know,' said Harriet impatiently. 'Perhaps Clay will see us, and we can shout. It will be daylight by then. If we stay here any longer, we'll never get to Clay in time.'

'All right,' agreed Aidan. 'Where do we go?'

At first, it was a tedious business of retracing their steps through the orchard and across the back yard. They dared not hurry, for fear of making too much noise, and rousing either Boz or Polly. But at last they reached the familiar track beyond the cowshed, and, disdaining the risk of a broken limb or a twisted ankle, they ran all the way to the Deacon's Flat road, with the patch of lamp-light dancing crazily before them.

'If we could wake Dinny up, she'd help us,' said Harriet, as they passed the O'Briens' cottage.

'We haven't got time,' panted Aidan. 'It must be after six already. We'll have to keep running.'

They found the Winneroo turn-off without difficulty, thanks to Harriet's keen observation, and jogged along the curving hill-side track beneath the she-oaks. Occasionally a rising breeze sent a cold shower of raindrops from the branches on to their heads, and they splashed through so many puddles that their boots were soon soaked. But Harriet was indifferent to these discomforts. She had forgotten her sorrow at the thought of leaving Lillipilly Hill, her uneasiness and her troubled conscience. All that mattered now was the rescue of Clay—the race with time, the mad running in the darkness and the loneliness, the feeling that she and Aidan were sharing an experience neither would forget, all combined to make her glow with warmth and exhilaration.

Even when they reached the gully where Dinny had spoken of leeches, Harriet barely paused. Aidan had to restrain her headlong rush.

'Don't be silly, Harriet—this part looks steep, and we don't know the way. You won't be any help to Clay if you break your neck. Let me go first.'

Forced to walk instead of run, Harriet began to

look about her, and to realize that trees, rocks, and scrubby bushes were emerging from the uniform blackness, and taking shape. Glancing up, she saw that the sky was a pale grey, and lined with low, wispy cloud.

'Aidan, it's getting light. What's the time?'

'A quarter to seven,' announced Aidan, dragging his watch from inside his damp and muddy jacket. 'The sun must be up by now. I expect the men will have left.'

In unspoken agreement, they began to run again. As they reached the top of the slope, it was light enough for them to discern the faint path that led seawards. The air was now alive with the pulsing of the waves, and distant white flecks on the misty horizon showed that a heavy sea was running. But they had only a fleeting glance to spare for this view—their gaze was fixed on the broad arm of the swamp that lay between them and Maloney's Hill.

'It's a long way,' said Harriet, her voice flat with despair. 'He'd never hear us from here.'

'We can try,' said Aidan, and they shouted together, startling themselves with the noise in that deserted spot, and raising echoes that mocked their efforts. No other voice answered them.

'We'll have to stop,' said Aidan at last. 'The men might be close enough to hear us. It's nearly seven.'

They stared again at the swamp. It was at least a quarter of a mile wide, criss-crossed with reed-beds, and studded with sprawling mangroves. Normally it was little more than a mud-flat, a sleepy backwater easily crossed, but today it too had been fed by the heavy rains, and it was impossible to guess its depth.

'There's only one thing we *can* do,' said Aidan. 'I don't think it's very deep. I can see lots of logs and roots sticking out.'

'You go first,' said Harriet. 'And if I can't follow, you go on without me. When we get closer, Clay might see us.'

They paused again for a moment at the edge of the swamp. The sky had turned from grey to red, and its stormy, unfriendly light glowered upon the water. Harriet glanced across at the dark hump of Maloney's Hill, and her imagination already peopled it with relentless armed figures. Grasping Aidan's hand—he had abandoned the lamp—she waded into the thick mud. Something moved under her foot, and she shuddered.

'Eels,' said Aidan. 'They won't hurt you.'

He was watching the water rising slowly and steadily up over his boots. Fortunately, the mud was quite firm, and gave way only very slightly beneath his tread. He had read enough adventure stories to be aware of the dangers of quicksand.

'There's a log here,' he said, prodding a submerged object with his foot. 'I'll pull you up on to it.'

The tree which had fallen there must have been quite a giant in its time, for it led them many yards out towards the centre of the swamp. When at last Aidan felt it narrowing, and offering a more and more precarious foothold, Maloney's Hill loomed very much closer.

'I don't think we'd better shout any more,' he said. 'The men would be sure to hear us. We'll try and reach those trees over there—it's not far.'

He lowered himself carefully from the log. The water swirled around his boot-tops, and he looked back anxiously at Harriet.

'At least,' said Harriet, with satisfaction, 'I shan't be able to wear this dress again.'

The trees Aidan had indicated were a group of mangroves, slender, twisted shapes with their heads close together, and their tangled roots half in and half out of the water. Beyond them, the swamp seemed shallower, and Aidan was confident that once they were in the mangroves' shelter, the worst part of the crossing would be over.

But Harriet was beginning to tire. She was

thoroughly chilled, and with every step her boots seemed heavier and colder. Once the sun peered through the clouds and glinted on the water, but there was no warmth in the pale, slanting light. It soon retreated, leaving the swamp more desolate and cheerless than before. Even the birds seemed to have fled from the backwater, and all around Harriet no living object was in sight, save her brother. Aidan floundered grimly on, still possessed with the idea of rescuing Clay, and determined that nothing should stop him. To Harriet, however, the vision of Clay was fast becoming blurred and indefinite—the reality was the never-ending swamp, the cold, and her own vast weariness.

'We're nearly there,' said Aidan. 'All we have to do now is find a way through these trees, and cross a bit of a mud-patch. I think we might still be in time.'

Harriet reached out blindly and grasped a mangrove root. In her normal state of mind, she would have marvelled at the strangeness of these trees, whose gnarled and prolific roots formed tunnels and archways and caves above and below the surface of the water. But now it was a frightening sight, for the branches shut out the light, and the muddy water was black and still and utterly silent. It was difficult to see Aidan, who in his eagerness was keeping well ahead of her, and she could only try to follow the splashing sounds he made as he scrambled from one root to the next.

'Aidan!' she called at last. 'Don't go on without me. I'd rather stay with you. Aidan!'

But no one answered her. The noise of Aidan's progress died away among the trees, and she knew she was alone. She could see nothing but trees wherever she looked. She felt one foot slipping in the mud, and drew back just in time from the edge of a deep hole. A cavern opened before her, and her feverish imagination transformed it into the lair of some horrible monster, crouching among the skeleton-like roots. She tried to go back the way she had come, but every tree so closely resembled its neighbour that it was impossible to recognize any landmarks.

She was far too exhausted now to think clearly. The water dragged clammily at her skirts, and her legs were numb. Her one desire was to leave this terrifying spot, and she spent the last of her strength turning desperately from one tree to the next, and calling continuously in a voice that even to herself seemed feeble and futile in all that loneliness. At last she pulled herself up on to a bridge of roots, and lay there a foot or two above the water, shivering and crying. From very far away came the sound of a shot, and the deep barking of a dog, but Harriet had forgotten both

Clay and Patchy. Only two things mattered now—the failing strength of her grip upon the tree-trunk, and the depth of the black water beneath her.

12

A future for Lillipilly Hill

Aidan heard the shot just as he reached the foot of the hill. Believing that Clay's pursuers were already attempting to capture him, he threw all caution to the winds, and shouted at the top of his voice, scrambling up the slope as he did so.

'Clay! Come this way! I'll help you!'

A wildly excited Patchy bounded through the scrub, almost knocking Aidan off his feet when she recognized him. And behind her came a most unexpected little procession, far removed from the angry group of hunters that Aidan had envisaged. For the leader was none other than Mr Farmer, as unruffled and as calm as he might have been in the pulpit of his church. He was followed by a rosy and cheerful Charles, and last of all came Clay, somewhat confused, certainly, but totally unharmed and apparently in no danger whatsoever.

Aidan sat down abruptly on the nearest rock.

'Is Clay all right?' he asked, quite unnecessarily.

'It seems that a number of people are bent on rescuing Clay this morning,' said Mr Farmer. 'Half Barley Creek is out looking for him. The shot you heard was Charles's signal for the search-party to be called off.'

'I don't understand any of it,' said Aidan, with the crossness produced by anti-climax. Then he glanced back down the hill.

'Where's Harriet? Has anyone seen her?'

'Harriet?' said Mr Farmer in alarm. 'Was she with you?'

'I thought she was following me. She must be still in the swamp,' and Aidan leapt away down the slope, terror giving him such speed that the others could hardly keep up with him.

Clay and Patchy found Harriet, for the mangrove clump was familiar territory to them, and Clay made his way through the tangled roots with the agility of an eel. Harriet still clung to her perch, blue with cold, and barely conscious.

'Take her home at once,' said Mr Farmer, as Clay and Aidan carried her to dry land. 'Charles, you help Clay. Aidan and I will follow you.'

'She won't get ill, will she?' asked Aidan. 'It's all my fault—she shouldn't have come.'

'I'm sure she only needs warmth and a rest,' the minister assured him. 'Now suppose we get all this straightened out as we go. Then perhaps I can help explain matters to your father.'

So Aidan told his story, not without shame and a gloomy feeling that his deeds were far from heroic when viewed by the cold, clear light of day.

'I thought the most important thing was to save Clay,' he finished. 'I didn't know it would be so dangerous.'

'You should have told your father, of course,' said Mr Farmer briskly. 'But never mind that now. Fortunately Charles brought the story of the man-hunt home from school, and I decided that the best thing to do would be to get to Clay before any harm was done. I persuaded the men not to approach him until I'd spoken to him. When I'd decided that Clay was certainly no criminal, then we gave the signal for everyone to go home.'

'So Harriet and I were no help at all,' said Aidan dismally.

'You at least proved that Clay had two loyal friends,' said Mr Farmer. 'He has been in need of friends for a long time.'

'Do you know all about him, then?' asked Aidan eagerly.

'I think I know most of it. His name is Clayton Stewart, and he must be sixteen or seventeen—he's a little vague about that. His father is an Englishman, of good family, but with not much else to recommend him, as far as I can judge. He married a half-aborigine girl who had much more character than he did. They lived in Blackhill for a time, then Clayton Stewart the elder set off up the country, carrying his swag, and has never come back. Mrs Stewart was left with four children to bring up—Clay is the oldest. She works as a maid in the hotel, and has the younger children with her, but Clay left the place because the hotel owner wouldn't let him keep his dog there. He's been living in his cave for about a year now, visiting his mother occasionally. He's never done anything wrong, I'm sure, but he preferred not to become known in case someone tried to send him back to his home—if you could call it a home. I don't really think anyone would have bothered—his mother has quite enough on her hands without Clay, and he's considered quite old enough to fend for himself. But there you are—he told

225

me all this to prove he wasn't the thief everyone was looking for, and his cave is hardly a secret any more.'

'What will he do now, then?' demanded Aidan.

'He doesn't know. He likes the open air, and his freedom. He will probably move to some other district, and live much the same sort of life. But it seems rather a pity—he's a pleasant sort of fellow, with nothing to be ashamed of, and good, steady employment with the right sort of people would make a fine man of him.'

Aidan said little for the rest of the way home—a roundabout way over the hills—but an idea had come to him, and helped to distract his thoughts from the subject of Harriet, a limp bundle being borne on the linked arms of Clay and Charles.

As they reached the eastern slope of Lillipilly Hill, the sun broke through the clouds in a widening patch of pale blue, and the soaked and battered countryside took on a fresh and glistening beauty. The lillipilly trees shook off their raindrops, and their polished, dark green leaves glittered in the sun. Beyond them, the old stone house was solid and square and ready to welcome all comers beneath its spreading roof.

'Such a fine old house,' said Mr Farmer. 'And one day it will probably be yours, Aidan. What will you do with it?'

Aidan considered this question with a feeling of

pleasure. He had never until now thought of himself as the future master of Lillipilly Hill—a few months ago, the vision would have been merely ridiculous. This morning, for the first time, he began to understand something of his father's pride in his possession.

'I shall have to think about it,' he said. 'But I'm sure I would never sell it. Perhaps I shall just live here, with Harriet to keep house, and I shall write books. Someone else would have to do the farming, because I don't think I shall ever be very good at that.'

They crossed the veranda, and for the next few minutes such a medley of explanations, exclamations, and instructions ensued that Aidan felt utterly exhausted, and crept away to his bed. He waited long enough, however, to see Harriet revived, and hear her demanding, 'Where's Clay? Did someone shoot him?' Once Clay had been brought forward for her inspection, she allowed herself to be taken off to her room and alternately fussed over and scolded by Polly, and for the rest of the morning she slept in the delicious comfort and warmth of her own safe bed.

Late in the afternoon, she sat up and looked out through the open door. The sky had cleared at last, and a gentle primrose-yellow light filled the air. Her father came along the veranda, smoking his pipe, and stood in the doorway.

'I hope you are quite recovered, Harriet. No coughs or sneezes?'

'I feel awfully well,' said Harriet gloomily. 'I wish I didn't.'

Her father advanced into the room to consider this rather unexpected statement.

'Do you think it would be more suitable to be ill, then?'

'If I were ill, then everyone would feel sorry for me, and do just as I wanted,' explained Harriet. 'But I shall have to get up as usual tomorrow, and then people will start saying it was all my own fault, and I should never have gone off with Aidan. And Mother will think we should go back to London after all.'

'Well, now, let me see,' said Mr Wilmot, sitting down on the edge of her bed. 'Some of those statements are quite true. You certainly should not have gone with Aidan—nor should Aidan have asked you to go. You should have both come to me with the whole story. However, you went this time with quite a sound reason, and your mother fully understands how much you wanted to help Clay. She thinks it was all very foolish and dangerous, of course, but as you have already suffered for your sins, we shall say no more about it.'

'Then Mother doesn't want to take us back to England?' asked Harriet incredulously.

'I don't believe we shall go back for a long time, Harriet. And when we do, it will probably be only a visit. We have decided, in the last few weeks, that when all is said and done, this is not a bad place in which to bring our family up. Your mother is very much stronger than she was, and the three of you have never looked healthier—that is, unless you have made up your mind to go into a decline. I would certainly advise you to keep away from swamps in future.'

Harriet shuddered.

'I'll never go near that place again. And I really don't feel a bit ill—I think I could jump right over the top of those bluegums. May I get up now?'

'Tomorrow will do nicely. Polly is bringing your tea in a moment, and Aidan is coming to present a formal apology for involving you in his wild schemes. So I shall leave you to enjoy yourself.'

When he had gone, Harriet continued to stare out at the tranquil garden and the darkening bush, feeling all the deep and humble relief of one who has been awakened from a bad dream.

'Tea-oh!' called Polly from the sliprail. 'Come and get it while it's hot. I'm not going to stand here all day!'

As always, someone hastened to do Polly's bidding. This time it was Dinny, scuffling through the furrows in her sturdy boots, for in mid-September it was still too early for her to go barefoot.

'Hot scones,' she observed with satisfaction, peering into Polly's basket. 'Two each, ain't there?'

'You must of learned something at that school, then,' said Polly. 'Mind you share them out proper, now.'

Dinny walked carefully back down the orchard, with the basket in one hand and the huge steaming billy of tea in the other. A strangely assorted group of tree-planters eagerly awaited her—Mr Wilmot and Boz, Aidan and Clay, Harriet and Rose-Ann. Along the hillside stretched a row of young trees, some three feet high, glossy-leaved and proudly bearing their clusters of pearly blossom. Near by, at the fence, stood one of Mr Bentley's drays, loaded with more trees ready for their new home. Bees hummed about them, and inquisitive peewits hopped among the graceful little branches.

The workers took their cups from the basket, held them out to be filled, and sought a brief resting place on the stone of the Ruins. Above them the sky was a clear blue; beyond the orchard the hills were sharp-edged in the still, fresh spring air. Already the weather was hinting at summer warmth and dryness, but meantime this was the proudest time of the year for the usually sober countryside—the bush slopes glowed with the gold of late wattles and wild broom, and the scarlet of the military waratah and the soldier-vine, while in more secret places bloomed the soft flannel-flower and the dainty bush-orchid. Harriet had gathered a great bunch of flowers only yesterday, and presented them to her mother.

'Those trees of Mr Bentley's are excellent stock,' said Mr Wilmot, surveying his new orchard with intense pleasure. 'We shall have to keep our first fruit for him.'

'They don't look too bad,' remarked Boz, and that was praise indeed.

'I've put labels on mine,' said Rose-Ann. 'Then when they have grown, I'll be able to eat my own oranges.'

'You won't be allowed to eat too many,' said Aidan. 'We're going to sell them, and make our fortune, aren't we, Father?'

'Not a fortune, just enough to make us comfortable,' corrected Mr Wilmot. 'This is not a country where fortunes are easily made.'

Clay whistled to Patchy, who was hunting rabbits on the other side of the fence. She came to gulp her share of scones, and lay down contentedly between Clay and Rose-Ann. Only to these two did she offer any affection, although she tolerated the presence of the others—she had to, now that she and Clay lived in a corner of Boz's shack. For Clay had found a home for both of them, and in return he worked tirelessly in the orchard, the garden, and the vegetable patch, and no longer mourned for his lost cave on Maloney's Hill. So great was his industry that even Boz had been heard to utter a word or two of approval.

'She's not a bad ole dog, is she?' said Dinny, who was enjoying her day with the Wilmots immensely—helping with the planting was certainly preferable to toiling in her own yard. 'An' people used to think she was a bunyip!'

'They thought Clay was a thief, too,' said Harriet, still full of indignation. 'And all the while it was that horrible man from the mill—what's his name, Dinny?'

'Alf Turner. Well, they've caught him good and proper now, an' everyone says he was always meant to come to a bad end. Trust Paddy to make such a stupid mistake. I'm glad Paddy's gone to Blackhill to that work on the railway—Barley Creek's much better without him.'

'Anyway, let's go and plant some more trees,' said Aidan. 'Charles is coming to help this afternoon, and then we're going to the cricket meeting. You're coming too, aren't you, Clay?'

Clay nodded assent, and one by one they returned to the row of trees, until Harriet was left alone. She had no intention of missing the planting, which to her was a solemn and pleasing ceremony, but she wanted, just for a moment, to savour all by herself the wonder of this spring morning, and the feeling, to be remembered all her life, that her dearest wishes had been lavishly granted. No princess in one of her fairy tales felt more blessed than Harriet, as she gazed upon the rich, brown soil and the brave young trees, and saw in her imagination the slopes bright with golden fruit.

'When the trees are bearing properly, I shall be a young lady, and Aidan will be quite grown-up,' she marvelled. 'And Dinny will have gone out to work, and Rose-Ann will be putting up her hair. Clay might even have a beard.'

She contemplated this fascinating vision for a few minutes.

'I might look like a young lady, but I shall feel just the same,' she decided at last. 'And anyway, what does it matter? When the oranges are ready to pick, we shall still all be here, and the year after that, and the next year—'

Dazzled by the prospect of the infinite and exciting time ahead, she cast one more glance at the quiet hills and the far-off sea, and ran to join the others.

Text Classics

Dancing on Coral
Glenda Adams
Introduced by Susan Wyndham

The Commandant
Jessica Anderson
Introduced by Carmen Callil

Homesickness
Murray Bail
Introduced by Peter Conrad

Sydney Bridge Upside Down
David Ballantyne
Introduced by Kate De Goldi

Bush Studies
Barbara Baynton
Introduced by Helen Garner

The Cardboard Crown
Martin Boyd
Introduced by Brenda Niall

A Difficult Young Man
Martin Boyd
Introduced by Sonya Hartnett

Outbreak of Love
Martin Boyd
Introduced by Chris Womersley

The Australian Ugliness
Robin Boyd
Introduced by Christos Tsiolkas

All the Green Year
Don Charlwood
Introduced by Michael McGirr

They Found a Cave
Nan Chauncy
Introduced by John Marsden

The Even More Complete
Book of Australian Verse
John Clarke

Diary of a Bad Year
J. M. Coetzee
Introduced by Peter Goldsworthy

Wake in Fright
Kenneth Cook
Introduced by Peter Temple

The Dying Trade
Peter Corris
Introduced by Charles Waterstreet

They're a Weird Mob
Nino Culotta
Introduced by Jacinta Tynan

The Songs of a Sentimental Bloke
C. J. Dennis
Introduced by Jack Thompson

Careful, He Might Hear You
Sumner Locke Elliott
Introduced by Robyn Nevin

Fairyland
Sumner Locke Elliott
Introduced by Dennis Altman

Terra Australis
Matthew Flinders
Introduced by Tim Flannery